CROSSROADS THROUGH THE HEART

Dixie Lynn Dwyer

MENAGE EVERLASTING

Siren Publishing, Inc.
www.SirenPublishing.com

A SIREN PUBLISHING BOOK
IMPRINT: Ménage Everlasting

CROSSROADS 4: SHOT THROUGH THE HEART
Copyright © 2016 by Dixie Lynn Dwyer

ISBN: 978-1-68295-790-5

First Printing: November 2016

Cover design by Les Byerley
All art and logo copyright © 2016 by Siren Publishing, Inc.

Printed in the U.S.A.

PUBLISHER
Siren Publishing, Inc.
www.SirenPublishing.com

DEDICATION

Dear readers,

Thank you for purchasing this legal copy of *Crossroads 4: Shot Through The Heart*.

Everyone has a gift, a talent, and ability that sets them apart from other people in the world. Discovering that gift, nurturing it, and feeding it so that you can excel and accomplish your life goals is a very tricky and difficult path sometimes.

Mia Mallory has such a gift—an ability to dissect a crime scene, view victims' bodies and evidence around that crime scene through the lens of her camera. But do not be fooled. Behind that strong, capable composure, is a woman suffering from loss, from heartache, and an experience that has hardened her heart and possibly even desensitized her to the evil, heinous crimes of truly violent perpetrators.

Yet somehow, in the midst of hunting a serial killer, paths cross, and love ignites so strong, so pure that not even the evil of one twisted mind can seem to destroy that love. Or can it?

May you enjoy the story.
Happy reading.
Hugs!
~Dixie~

CROSSROADS 4: SHOT THROUGH THE HEART

DIXIE LYNN DWYER
Copyright © 2015

Prologue

Her laughter was addicting. Her smile, her long brown hair, and her voluptuous figure were that of a goddess, not of some college co-ed. She didn't belong around those boys trying to act like men. They would hurt her, take from her innocence, and that couldn't happen.

He sipped his beer and watched her and her friends. It was almost time. Weekend after weekend he'd traveled into the city just to see her. To catch a glimpse and prepare himself to fulfill his fantasies with her. She would belong to him in every way. There were no others. No substitutes for her. He'd tried. He'd failed. He'd almost gone too far. He couldn't bring that kind of attention to himself. He had to maintain control of the emotions and desires.

He had tried unsuccessfully to get her off his mind. But the more he learned about her, saw her strength, her independence, and spirit, the more she appealed to him. She wasn't weak but, instead, strong and capable. He knew her parents. He'd seen them struggle with illness and also give her nothing but grief and pain. They were old. They weren't even her biological parents. She was adopted, like him. She was too old to be cared for and placed in another home but too sensual of a young woman to be left unguarded. That night he'd stopped that dirty social services guy from trying to manipulate her, trick her into getting into his car, was special. It had been the moment her gorgeous dark-blue eyes locked onto his and he saw everything he was searching for. Then she'd disappeared. Until now.

He guzzled down his beer and saw her look at her watch. She was a good girl, not a slut. She worked hard, studied hard, and barely went out, but next week, finals were over. When she came home, he would be there waiting. He would take her then. He had his plan. He had his house set up and everything ready, including the drugs to manipulate her mind and ease her ability to resist his charms and his games of pleasure because he knew she was innocent. She didn't trust easily. She hid from being the focus of attention. She would be his focus of attention, every day for the rest of their lives. His cock hardened, and his heart began to pound against his chest. He needed her so badly it hurt.

Mia, I'm coming for you. I've waited long enough.

Chapter 1

Mia Mallory rubbed her eyes, feeling the exhaustion of being at the computer for so long. But she couldn't sleep. Not with all that racket going on next door. She hated living here and really wanted to find a new apartment but just couldn't find the time to search. Plus, between Wellington and Portland Place, there were less apartments and more houses and cottages for sale. She wouldn't be comfortable living in a house or even a cottage alone, never mind in a heavily wooded area. Too many bad memories there.

She swallowed hard. Life had thrown her nothing but one curve ball after the next. She looked away from the computer and glanced up at the pictures on her desk. She didn't know why she even bothered to keep them. Nor the photo album filled with what seemed like a past life, a time and a place that existed when she was innocent, unknowing, untouched by the evil of society. The tears filled her eyes, but not like they had years ago. So instant, so full, she couldn't hide the tears that streaked down her cheeks. Her profession, her determination to live and move on, had desensitized her to things most people couldn't even imagine, never mind experience and see. Not everyone had the emotional and physical fortitude, much less the strength, to view dead bodies and photograph them at their crime scenes.

She stretched her muscles and saw the definition in them and the lightly raised veins against her wrist and forearms. She was in great physical condition, a black belt in Tae Kwon Do and expert in weapons, thanks not only to the police academy but to R.J.

She felt her chest tighten. She missed him. Despite them both knowing that being lovers wasn't ever going to work out, she still missed him. Those several months together after Wynona had been murdered had helped her get through losing her roommate and also compounded the desire to achieve her degree and help to capture individuals who took innocent people's lives.

She ran her finger along the small porcelain box, the one that held the locket he had given her that she no longer wore. She thought about the nights they'd spent going out to dinner and training on the mats at Sparrow's dojo in the city. It felt like a lifetime ago. Just like everything else in her life, no one stuck around. No one committed to her fully, only temporarily. It was because she had a hardened heart. She'd created a kind of barrier over it that ensured she showed little emotion or let anyone get close to her. It was lonely, but she was used to it. It hurt less than the pain of losing someone you'd given your heart to or even loved.

She felt guilty for feeling relieved that she was still alive when the police and the detectives like R.J. had told her she should be dead. Had that killer, the one who'd taken Wynona, been after her, too? She would never know. Just like she would never know why her biological parents had given her up for adoption and why her adoptive parents had to be so old they couldn't even live long enough to see her go to college.

She no longer felt sadness when she thought such things or feelings like worthlessness or being unneeded in this world, as though she was taking up space and would never be an asset to society, to anyone. Instead, she felt numb, as if she had gotten used to being truly alone and unconnected. Wasn't it easier than feeling?

Her only feelings of being connected or of fulfillment and making a difference came when she worked. Her ability to not only take the right pictures and document the evidence, but also assist in profiling the killers, was a gift, an innate ability, and also a curse. Too bad that gift hadn't been present when Wynona had been found murdered.

That had been a few years back before she completed her training and after she was forced into counseling by the department.

She shifted in her chair and stood up. She looked at the computer. Wynona's killer was still out there. She tightened her grip and thought about the search. She thought about the different avenues the detectives had focused on. They were all dead ends, even the fact that Wynona had been so drunk when she got back to the apartment that she'd slept in Mia's bed. Mia could have been killed, too, if she hadn't got caught up in a project at the academy. But to learn her own apartment had been turned into a crime scene, and men and women she knew, who had helped train her, had to photograph her apartment, look for fingerprints and evidence to find out who'd taken Wynona made her feel so violated and unsafe.

It had been all over the media and had sent the local colleges in the city into a panic. Extra security was added to campuses, and police patrols throughout the city late at night kept watch on the co-eds that drank at bars until early morning hours. It was insane, and then came the news of evidence. Some thirty minutes away in the woods a shoe was found. The search parties consisted of everyone from law enforcement to volunteers from the colleges and communities.

Hours upon hours they looked through the deep wooded area in Upstate New York. There were clues and evidence left behind. Pieces of clothing, a high-heel shoe, and even blood.

She was the one who'd discovered Wynona's body in the search through the woods. Mia would never forget that day. Only a state away in Pennsylvania, a place filled with deep woods and gorgeous works of art created by Mother Nature, and on a good day captured by the lens on her digital camera. Those woods also contained danger, isolation from society, and no one for miles. When she thought of the woods, she thought of Wynona's screams for help. The only witnesses to her last dying breaths had been the trees and wildlife within.

Mia shivered from the thoughts and walked away from her desk.

There was nothing she could do about it now, no way to ease the spirit of her friend or those who had passed before her, murdered, victims of violent, brutal crimes and heinous acts by monsters. Except for one way—capture them by catching their mistakes.

She looked at her camera bags that sat by the front door, ready to leave with her now. Nothing she could ever want for herself mattered. Nothing. She lived and breathed for that buzz on her phone in the morning or at any given hour when she got a call for work. This was her life. She hunted killers, and one day she would find Wynona's.

* * * *

Tiegen McKay stood near the security guards by the entrance of the terminal. He ground his teeth and tapped his foot, just staring down the hallway and waiting to see his brother appear or at least some people from the plane that had landed. The terminal was small. The whole airport was, which made it ideal for business travel and, of course, more common flights like from the military base in South Carolina. He couldn't wait to see his brother Murdock, especially knowing that he had a close call while on some damn mission for the government. Tiegen wished Murdock was a cop like him and Mitch, but then again, wearing blue was becoming almost as dangerous as wearing fatigues.

He took an uneasy breath as he glanced around him. He was always in cop mode, a state police investigator, a man that had seen some bad shit and the evil allowed to roam free on this earth. It all gave him nightmares and made him wonder if he could ever give it up. Ever stop hunting killers and bringing justice to people's families. Especially after the last week he had.

His eyes landed on his brother as he slowly walked up the small incline, limping and wearing dark sunglasses and fatigues, and carrying a duffel bag. He always traveled light. The closer Murdock got, the more Tiegen took in of his six-feet-four height, conditioned body, and trim waist. He was a walking killing machine.

"Murdock." He reached for him. His brother dropped his bag and held him close, slapping his hand against his back in a bear hug.

Tiegen chuckled and pulled back. The relief must have been apparent on his face because Murdock picked his bag back up, grunted, and looked at him. At least he thought he did, but the dark sunglasses covered his eyes. Tiegen could see the scrapes and bruises on his cheeks leading behind the glasses.

"What the hell happened? Are you okay?" he asked him as they started to walk.

"I'm alive, Tiegen," he said very flatly, and Tiegen swallowed hard.

They didn't say another word to one another until they got into the parking lot and to the truck. They were big men, tough men who didn't show emotion in public but who were closer than normal brothers by far. He would wait to see when Murdock was ready to talk. Once they were inside, Murdock leaned his head back and exhaled.

"Thanks for coming to get me."

"No problem, it was easy for me to head out of the city today early. It worked out just fine."

The silence continued, and so badly Tiegen wanted to ask Murdock what had gone down, but he knew he couldn't. His missions were always so secretive.

"How is Mitch?" he asked.

"He's busy with some case in Wellington. Some break-ins have been happening, and they started a few months ago. The perpetrators started expanding their territory from Wellington to Portland Place now. But he says he's getting close. I think he brought in Toro Vancouver to help."

Murdock turned to look at him and then chuckled. "Damn, he needs a tracker to find these punks."

"They committed a couple of home invasions. Put some residents in the hospital and nearly killed an older couple when they both sustained heart attacks. It's getting worse each time. Mitch thinks that they have a connection in both towns, a person who identifies the right people and homes to break into."

"Well, Mitch is like a pit bull. He never gives up until he gets what he's after."

"All three of us can be like that," Tiegen said and chuckled.

"Sometimes it's better to let go. We learned that, too."

Tiegen knew what he was talking about. LeeAnn. She wanted him to quit, to end his career with the service and go work for her father in the city in some firm of his. A white-collar guy was not who Murdock was. They were so different, and she wanted him to change to be the man she wanted. It had hurt his brother a lot, especially to return from a mission and find out LeeAnn was engaged.

"Well, we're both glad you're back home and in one piece. Do you want to hit Crossroads or someplace for dinner?"

"What about Mitch?"

"He'll meet us if he can."

"Okay, but not too long. I'm pretty damn tired, and I haven't had a decent meal in weeks."

"Well then, a nice porterhouse steak will be prefect, won't it?"

Murdock nodded but remained straight-faced. He was such a hard, tough man. Even his heart appeared to be made of Teflon, but Tiegen couldn't get upset. This was always how it was when Murdock first returned home. He was distant, quiet, and kept to himself until he felt he'd adjusted back to civilian life again. Tiegen was fine with that, as long as he came back in one piece and not in a body bag.

* * * *

Mitch got to the house along with members of the Criminal Investigation Unit. He noticed the multiple police cars, some paramedics, and, of course, how officers were taping off the area so local residents wouldn't get in the way.

He couldn't believe it. He had just gotten off the phone with Toro Vancouver, who'd gotten a potential clue to someone who may or may not be involved with these home invasions, when he got the call about another break-in and a homeowner found dead.

"Hey, Detective. Looks like these break-ins are getting worse," Officer Torey Welder said to him as he lifted the yellow tape so Mitch could get under.

"Everything taped off? No one touched anything?" he asked.

"No one. The forensics team got here five minutes ago."

He nodded toward the kid and headed up the walkway then inside. He bypassed the officers on guard and then made his way up the stairs.

As he approached, he caught sight of the markings, the little tabs where the forensics team had marked out blood spots and the damage to the walls. It appeared there had been a struggle.

As he approached the top of the stairs, he heard the clicking of a camera and then caught sight of Mia bending over to get a shot at an awkward angle.

"Great job, Mia. Be sure to follow them outside to the back woods," Jethro Shank told her. He was the medical examiner and was already pulling off his gloves after looking at the body. He glanced up just as Mia caught Mitch's eye.

She gave him a nod.

"Hey, Mia."

"Detective McKay." She then walked right by him. He followed her with his eyes and wondered what her attitude and tone were about, but then Jethro said hello.

"Damn shame. The perpetrators didn't think it was enough to kill him. They beat him first," Jethro said as Mitch looked around.

"That drawer was open," he said, moving closer and peaking inside.

"You can look. Mia got here before the rest of the team and took photos of everything. I bet that's what this poor guy was reaching for."

"A gun, huh? Wonder why the perps didn't take it."

"I think this homeowner got a few shots in on the guy's body."

Mitch widened his eyes. "The blood on the stairs and on the landing?"

"Could belong to the criminal. I'll know for sure later today once we compare DNA to this guy."

"Detective McKay, I was just talking to the neighbor down the road. Seems Mr. Phillips, the guy there, had his grandchildren over this weekend. We can't find them, and no one knows if they left town already or if they were still here with Mr. Phillips. They're six and eight years old."

"Shit, get the officers together and search the house. Have someone try to find a next of kin. Be careful. Look in every closet and in every space. Identify yourselves as police and remember they're probably scared if they are in the house." Mitch pulled out his cell and notified the others.

He headed through the hallways and began to help the officers search for the two kids, and then he went down the stairs.

* * * *

Mia had walked along the staircase to the first floor and around past the kitchen to find the back door. She heard a noise coming from behind one of the doors. She put down her camera bag and pulled her gun from the holster. Just as she opened the door, she heard officers coming down the hallway, and then she heard whispering and footsteps. She'd begun to walk down the stairs, gun drawn, when she sensed someone behind her. It was one of the officers.

"Did you hear something?" he whispered as he pulled his gun from the holster. She nodded and then continued to walk slowly.

Others joined them. At least she sensed that as she kept her eyes glancing around the stairs, trying to see in the poorly lit basement. The only light shown through the small window toward the back of the basement.

She listened carefully. She heard what sounded like sniffling and low crying sounds.

"Is anyone down here? I'm with the police."

She heard the word no, whispered sharply. It sounded like a kid's voice.

She looked at Torey. "There were two grandkids supposedly in the house with the grandfather. We think four and six years old. They're unaccounted for." Torey told her.

Her heart pounded. Jesus, they'd probably heard the struggle and gone to hide. They knew their grandfather was killed. Damn it. They must be so scared.

She caught sight of Mitch as he came down the stairs behind two other officers. She raised her hand up for them to stop, and he looked at her as if she was nuts. Or maybe wondering who the hell she was to give orders. But something came over her. Call it knowing what fear like this was, or simply knowing firsthand what it was like to be the one that got away unharmed while someone else died.

"My name is Mia. I'm one of the good guys, and we're here to help you. Come on out and we'll talk."

She heard a sound, like shoes shuffling against concrete.

"I'm scared." She heard the female voice and what sounded like crying.

"I know you are. It's safe now."

Mia began to walk closer.

"Mia." She heard Mitch say her name with authority. She ignored him, placed her gun in her holster, and moved deeper into the basement, and then she saw them. A boy and a girl, no older than maybe eight if she had to guess. She bent to one knee and opened her arms.

"You're safe. Come to me and I'll help you. I promise."

They were both crying and shaking and slowly came out from under the desk. She saw the bloody lip on the boy, and then they both hugged her and held on tightly as they cried.

Mia fell to her butt and held them close. She rocked them in her arms and swallowed the lump of emotion in her throat. She couldn't say anything to them. She just held them because anything she said would be a lie. "It's going to be okay now" or "you'll get through this just fine" or "it's behind you" were all lies. They would live with this tragedy forever, but hopefully, they were young enough to not get all fucked up. She hadn't been so lucky.

* * * *

Mitch watched as the paramedics had to peel the two kids from Mia's arms. Mia was good though. She stayed right by them, caressing their cheeks and acting so caring and nurturing. But the moment the kids calmed down and Mitch was forced to ask them questions, it seemed that Mia got a bit on the defensive.

"Did you see who broke into the house?" he asked, even though they wouldn't verbally respond to his other questions and, instead, nodded or shook their heads. Mia sat between them on the gurney. They kept their heads against her side as she held them.

"Maybe this can wait," she said with a defensive tone. He squinted at her as the other officers and detective stood by.

"You know it can't. It's fresh in their heads, and they could describe the ones who did it."

"We need answers," another detective, Davie, said. Mitch looked at him and then back at Mia.

"Let me," she whispered.

He stared at her. His gut clenched. There was something going on here. Something deeper that seemed to have a hold of Mia. He looked at Jethro, who placed his hand on Davie's shoulder.

"Mitch, let Mia help you."

Mitch nodded toward the other men, dismissing them from the area except for Davie.

"Cassy, Luke, I know this is hard, but these detectives want to help find the men that broke into the house," she said to them.

"They killed Grandpa," Cassy said and began to cry again. She was shaking, and Mia hugged her.

"I know, baby, and we want to catch them so they can't hurt anyone else."

"There were two men," Luke said to her. Mitch felt his stomach clench. He had figured two.

"Did you get a good look at them?" she asked, and Cassy and Luke nodded.

"Could you draw them?" she asked.

"I don't know."

"What are they going to draw? Mickey Mouse?" the other detective asked, and Mia shot him a dirty look.

Mitch switched from one foot to the other and looked at her.

"Pen and paper?" she asked, and Mitch nodded toward the other detective, who pulled out a pad and paper.

"Okay, let's start with the first guy. What color hair did he have?"

Mitch listened to her, watching her get information from two little kids with ease and perfection. The other detective watched with surprise, and Mitch had to hide his smile. It turned out that Mia was pretty damn good at this.

"Do you remember if they had any distinguishing marks, like moles, or tattoos, a scar or damaged skin?" she asked.

"The one who tried to chase us had a scar by his eye and a chain hanging from his jeans to his pocket. Like the ones for wallets so you don't lose them," Cassy said to her. She smiled at the children and got more information.

"I saw the truck they drove," Luke told her, and Mitch couldn't believe it. He listened as Mia calmly talked to the two children, getting details he knew he or Davie, the other detective, would have had a hard time getting, or may have failed entirely.

Then they heard some voices and Cassy cry out. The grandmother and mother arrived, and the children got down and ran to them.

He locked gazes with Mia and saw the emotion in her eyes, and then their gazes locked, and he was amazed. She'd closed down, her expression blank as she handed him the papers with all the details, including a partial license plate on the truck.

She started to walk away.

"Mia." He touched her arm lightly, stopping her.

"I need to photograph the woods and outside the back door."

"You were incredible."

She nodded, and he released her arm, even though he didn't want to. He really wanted to hold her, pull her into his arms, and hug her for what she'd done and how much of a blessing she was to those kids and an asset to the job. But then he felt that attraction, the desire to get to know her more. He watched her as she headed past Davie and the others and over to Jethro, who gave her a smile and then followed her inside the house.

"Damn, she was something else. I've never seen anything like it," Davie said to him.

"You weren't going to let her continue with the kids. There's no way we would have gotten what she did."

"It would have taken longer, but eventually I could have. She's not even a detective."

"She could be."

"Maybe. I'm going to grab this info and get things started. If any of the other residents down the road have security cameras, they might have caught sight of this truck our killers took off in. But even if they didn't, we have this partial license plate number. I can't believe those kids would remember such details."

"I know. Pretty damn amazing and so was Mia."

Davie nodded then headed over to the other police officers and began to give orders of what needed to be done next. Mitch walked over to the grandmother and mother of the two kids. He had some questions for them but hoped to get an opportunity to talk to Mia again and to thank her.

* * * *

Mia finished taking the pictures. She forced the memories from her past to the back of her mind for later. She was always professional, always put the job first, and knowing that those two kids suffered and could have died was incentive to do things right.

She squatted down and took some notes as the other technicians began to pack up. As she got her camera and lenses into the bag, she couldn't help but wonder about how this happened and how the kids got away. It wasn't her job to ask questions, but where had the mother and grandmother been the whole time this home invasion was happening? She thought about their facial expressions and the way they ran to the kids as they approached the ambulance. The mother of the children was crying hysterically, but the grandmother just looked scared, not upset. It didn't sit right with Mia, but what did she know? She didn't even have a family.

Before she stood, she closed her eyes and absorbed the moment of quietness. That was when the flashbacks hit her. The dark woods, so much brush and thickness of trees that evidence could have gone unnoticed. She was concentrating so hard at the time and wondering if her friend suffered. She couldn't help but imagine the echoing of screams no one heard. When she stepped through the heavy brush, deep in the woods, a good fifteen to twenty feet between her other searchers, she'd stumbled over her dead friend's body.

"Mia?"

She gasped and nearly lost her balance. Quickly, she stood up and wiped off her pants as the hand gripped her arm and helped steady her.

"Are you okay?" Mitch asked, and she nodded.

"Just being clumsy." She brushed off his concern as she stared up at him. He was a very attractive older man, with dark hair and deep dark-blue eyes and scruff along his chin and cheeks. He was hard, in charge, and a typical homicide detective.

"You sure?" he asked, hesitating to release her arm. He held her gaze as he slowly released his hold and then caressed her skin. She shivered with an awareness she hadn't expected. It seemed each time she met up with Mitch she had this feeling. But she also had the same feelings for his brother Tiegen, who she hadn't seen in months. Not since the serial killer and all those bodies.

She cleared her throat and then plastered on a smile.

"Did you need anything?" she asked him, and he looked at her with an expression that said he read her fake smile as bullshit.

"You sure you're okay? That was some heavy emotional shit back there."

She shrugged. "I hate to admit that it wasn't my first case of heavy emotional shit at a crime scene."

"Really? So you always are able to comfort survivors and get them to remember crucial facts that can help detectives find the perpetrators?" he teased.

She pursed her lips and then pulled the bottom lip between her teeth before she spoke. "I just did what needed to be done. They were pretty scared, and Davie tends to come on like a German shepherd sometimes when he's questioning witnesses."

He chuckled.

"He would love being called a German shepherd. He was a bit too rough but glad you were there and heard those kids downstairs. They seemed to respond immediately to you."

"It's not a big deal. So did you get anything useful? Maybe that description of the vehicle and the license plate?"

"Davie is working on it now. How about you? Get enough pictures?"

"I think so, but something tells me you won't be needing them."

"I wouldn't say that. You were a huge help, and I appreciate it. So do I get another thumb drive of these pictures for me to look over?"

"Sure. I can put one together for you once I get back to the office. I can drop it off with Jethro, and when you guys go to the morgue, he'll give it to you."

He looked at her and then looked around him as if being sure no one could hear him.

"I was kind of hoping maybe you'd give it to me personally. Perhaps we could meet up for coffee or lunch this week?"

She looked away from him. So badly she would love to feel normal and say yes, but how could she? She'd already made the mistake of getting involved with RJ, an older man, detective, and retired soldier. What a mess she'd made of that relationship because she couldn't let her guard down and trust the man enough to let him in her heart.

"I don't think that's a good idea."

He placed his hand on his holster and leaned slightly. "Why not?"

"Because we sort of work together and I don't date. I don't have the time or the patience for it." She readjusted the strap to the camera bag, onto her shoulder.

"Don't have the time for it? Never heard that excuse before, and as far as working together? We don't, so no issues there. What do you say to coffee? I know you drink it. I saw you."

She gave a soft smile. "I'll think about it, okay?"

"I'll get you to say yes," he said, and then she heard someone call her name. It was another technician, and he said they were wrapping things up."

"I'll see you tomorrow then," he said to her.

"Later, Mitch, and thank you."

"No, thank you, Mia. You were a huge help today."

She headed away from the back of the house and over to the truck. She couldn't help but to look for Mitch and take in the sight of him. He had a super great body, was tall, muscular, and seemed very capable. He affected her. That was for sure. But the thought of trying to let her guard down and let a man into her life truly freaked her out. She couldn't meet him for coffee. No way. She was better off alone. Look how things had gone so wrong with R.J. Sure, he had his issues, too, but she was more screwed up. She shook the sad thoughts from her head and looked back at the house one last time. Her worry was the kids.

They'd been present when their grandfather was murdered. They'd hidden in the darkness of a basement, heard all the chaos going on upstairs, and then even hid from police. It was traumatic and would stay with them forever. Maybe she would come back to see them again tomorrow. She understood what it was like to witness such violence. She thought about Wynona. Why couldn't she just let it go and start living her life?

Because her killer is still out there. Perhaps he's even struck again, and that's why I can't stop thinking about Wynona.

Chapter 2

Murdock walked into the kitchen, pulling on a hooded sweatshirt. It was cold this morning. The fall temperatures were beginning to feel more like winter. He couldn't sleep and had heard one of his brothers up before the crack of dawn and then smelled the scent of fresh-brewed coffee.

"Shit, did I wake you?" Mitch asked, looking up from the kitchen table. He held a dark cobalt-blue mug in his hand.

"Nah. Couldn't sleep." He opened the cabinet door to pull out his own mug, the same color as Mitch's, and then poured himself a cup.

"Sorry I couldn't meet you at the airport with Tiegen or at Crossroads for dinner."

"No problem. I'll be here for a while. We'll get some time to hang out."

Mitch nodded and then ran his hand along his shoulder as if trying to unknot tight muscles.

"You okay?" Murdock asked him then took a sip of hot black coffee. It eased down his throat and slowly began to take away the chill of the early morning.

"Just a bad case. Thought we had good enough evidence to catch these guys, and it's like they disappeared off the face of the earth."

"Does this have something to do with the home invasions?"

Mitch nodded. "There have been over six in the past few months. They've gotten worse, and yesterday a man was killed, and his grandchildren were in the house."

Murdock squinted his eyes and pursed his lips, appearing angry. "Were the kids hurt, too?"

Mitch shook his head.

"They hid in the basement."

"Shit."

"I know it was bad, but we wound up getting a lot of information from them, including a make of the truck, a partial license plate, and full description."

"Seriously? After something so traumatic like that?"

Mitch nodded, and then he ran his finger along his coffee mug.

"A forensics photographer got the kids to open up to her. She was incredible."

Murdock heard something different in Mitch's voice.

"You know this forensics photographer well?" he asked, and Mitch looked up.

"Worked with her a few times."

He got quiet, and Murdock wondered why.

"Davie was going to question the kids. Came across off intense and confrontational like he would with an adult. She stepped in, and that was it. The kids instantly trusted her, leaned on her, and she did her thing. Got full descriptions and it was impressive."

"Davie has always acted like an attack dog."

"Yeah, well, Mia put him in his place fast. Anyway, I'm heading into Yarland this morning to check out this one location Toro found out about. Seems these guys that match the description of our perps help run a scrap metal business there. Some shady characters around."

"You going alone?"

Mitch stood up to pour another cup of coffee.

"Don't have much choice. We're all working on any leads we get in, and the manpower is low with two guys leaving town."

"I can go with you if you want."

Mitch turned to look at him and then gave a small smile.

"Yeah?"

"Sure. I won't be heading to the dojo in Portland until later in the week anyway."

"Okay, we leave in thirty. That good?"

"No problem." Murdock swallowed the last sip of coffee from his mug.

"Where is Tiegen?"

"Beats the hell out of me. He never came in last night."

"It's pretty disheartening to know there are so many fucked-up people out there that you guys are always out investigating."

"Says the soldier who's always leaving for another assignment."

"It gets tiring after a while. Leaving you guys, risking my neck for shit and half the time I don't even know why."

Mitch looked at him and nodded. "You've served your country, and you've gone through heavy shit. Some recently if those scratches on your cheeks and bruise by your eye are any indication. But hey, anytime you want to come join Tiegen and me in the family business you let me know. I've got connections in the department."

Murdock chuckled. "We at this again, Mitch?"

"I'll keep trying to get you to stay here in Wellington where you belong."

"More like where you can keep an eye on me?"

"Well, that too. But like you're getting tired of fighting for things and risking your life for things you don't even know about, Tiegen and I are getting tired of seeing you leave and wondering if you'll return home in one piece or at all."

Murdock swallowed hard and felt the tightness in his chest. He had been feeling the same way lately, as though perhaps it was time to retire from the military. He'd let his commander know he was considering it before he headed home this time. His commander understood.

"I've been thinking about it, too, Mitch."

Mitch smiled. "Maybe after today, and you see how cool it is to be a detective, you'll want to follow in my footsteps. I can teach you the ropes."

Murdock chuckled. "I think I may be the one to teach you a thing or two. I've got training you couldn't even imagine."

"Ohh…starting that shit, huh? Okay, Special Forces, we'll see."

Murdock chuckled and then put his mug in the sink.

Then he felt Mitch's hand on his shoulder. He looked at his brother, instantly feeling that deep connection and bond that he, Mitch, and Tiegen had shared since forever.

"I'm glad you're home. Everything feels right when the three of us are here and in one piece." Then he released his shoulder and walked away before the emotions got to him.

Murdock watched him walk out of the room.

He had some decisions to make, and he hoped he could handle civilian life and one day could feel normal instead of feeling like a professional killer.

* * * *

Mia was a little nervous about visiting the two kids, Cassy and Luke. But once she was inside their home and saw their huge smiles right before they ran to hug her, she was relieved. She talked to them about regular things and about being strong. They shared stories about their grandpa and showed her pictures, too. That was when Mia noticed the sign behind their grandfather in one of the pictures.

"Your dad was a financial advisor?" she asked their mother, Courtney.

She took the picture from Mia's hand and nodded. "He did that for years, but he suffered a heart attack last year and decided that the stress was too much for him. But my dad loved working, so he took on some clients locally. But not too many."

She nodded. "And your mom?"

"My mom is into art galas and collecting antiques. In fact my father purchased that house in Portland Place because their smaller house in Yarland is filled with antiques and things. She liked throwing parties there though, so she could show off her collection."

"I like antiques, too," Mia said.

"Do you collect as well?" Courtney asked her.

"No. I live in an apartment right now, and the antiques that always catch my eye are out of my price range." Mia chuckled.

"That never stopped my mom from buying pieces. I remember my dad would get so upset with her and say she was spending their retirement savings on furniture." The tears filled Courtney's eyes, and she wiped them away then looked toward the kids.

Mia placed her hand over Courtney's. "You'll get through this."

She nodded and then held Mia's gaze. "You were so good with the kids. I couldn't even imagine what they'd gone through. I can't even sleep at night knowing what they experienced and heard. I can't grasp the fact that my father is gone."

"That's understandable. The best thing to do is to be there for them and to talk to them. I don't know if anyone left you any papers or anything, but I brought along this paperwork on a counseling service that's great for families, especially for kids. An art therapy type of thing. It may be helpful." Mia placed the paper down onto the table, and Courtney smiled.

"Thank you so much, Mia."

As Mia left the house and got into her car, she couldn't help the ideas and questions that were spinning through her mind. She headed out of the driveway and then made the left instead of the right to head back to Portland Place. Instead, she headed into Yarland.

In one of the pictures of the kids' grandparents, they were standing in front of a piece of furniture and behind them was a delivery van. The letters that she could make out were "RLAND." Other letters were missing, but she thought perhaps they were "YA" and together spelled out YARLAND.

As she made her way through the winding roads and into town, she admired the beauty of another small town and all it had to offer the locals and even tourists. There was an antique store, a small grocery store, and other little places, but despite the size, it had an upscale look to it. Even the buildings coordinated with the landscaping and the colors of burgundy and gold in the flowers. The fall colors with mums and cabbage in planters looked appealing against the backdrop of large trees with yellow, orange, and red leaves in abundance.

It was when she passed a small side street that something white caught her eye. She stopped, put on her signal, and made the turn. As she slowly drove closer, three things hit her simultaneously.

One was the white van with the words YARLAND Deliveries on it sitting outside of a building that had no name on it but looked old with one large garage bay. Two was the sight of Mrs. Phillips handing over an envelope, appearing as if she was giving orders and rushing the men along. Mia's gut clenched. She thought it looked suspicious and wasn't certain why. Maybe because her husband just died so why would she be out here? It didn't seem right, and Mia followed her gut instincts and looked at the men. There were three of them, two of whom looked like the description of the men who'd broken into the house and killed Mr. Phillips. She couldn't be sure unless she got closer, but the one guy lifting things into the back of the van had a chain hanging from his front pocket to his back pocket, just as Cassy and Luke described. This was more than coincidence. She just knew it.

Mia's stomach tightened, and she pulled to the side, hoping they hadn't noticed her. She wondered what she should do. She thought about Mitch and reached for her cell phone. If this were a case of foul play, she would need backup and quickly. They looked about ready to leave.

* * * *

Mitch was laughing at something Murdock said when his cell phone rang. They were about five minutes outside of Yarland. He saw the caller ID and smiled then felt that instant tightness in his chest. It was Mia.

"McKay."

"Mitch, it's Mia. I'm in Yarland. I was in Portland Place visiting the kids and Mr. Phillips's daughter when they were showing me pictures and…"

He listed to what she was saying and tried following her rambled speech.

"So you think that the wife was involved?" he asked.

"The wife is here right now, I believe with the two guys that match the description the kids gave, and there's a third guy, too. Did you know that Mr. Phillips was a financial advisor? That his wife collects expensive antiques?"

"We pulled a lot of info together last night. Where are you exactly? I don't want you to make a move without us."

"Us?"

"My brother Murdock is with me."

"He's a cop, too?"

"No, but he's carrying. Just sit tight. I'll be there in a matter of seconds.

"Shit, they're starting to leave. I have to stop them. Come to High Avenue."

"Mia," he exclaimed and then heard the phone click off. He explained what was going on to Murdock and then gave him the number for the Yarland police to respond.

As he pulled along the side street, he found High Avenue then he caught sight of Mia surrounded by the three men, two of which were holding large sticks or bats. He also saw an older woman getting into her car and trying to reverse out of the parking spot.

"Oh fuck."

He slammed his car into the older woman's vehicle, and Murdock jumped out of the passenger side of the car.

It happened so quickly. He caught sight of the older woman leaning her head against the steering wheel, obviously hurt. Then he saw Mia defending herself as two men struck at her and she fought back, knocking one down with a high kick and another with a forearm to the throat, but the third struck her across the mouth and then grabbed her, wrapped his arms around her arms and midsection, and lifted her up in a bear hug.

"Stop. Police. Let her go," he yelled as Murdock knocked out one guy with one punch to the nose. He reached for the other guy, and Mitch went for the one holding Mia. But Mia took that moment to slam her head backward, causing the guy's nose to break and splatter blood as he released her. She turned and jabbed him in the scrotum. The guy went down to his knees and then slammed his arm against her legs, knocking her onto her back. Mitch tackled the guy to the ground, turned him over, and cuffed him.

The sound of sirens blaring and cars pulling up quickly alerted them that help had arrived.

Mitch turned to look at Mia, who was slow to get up, her lip bleeding. There was dirt all over her blouse and pants.

"Are you okay?" He used his knee to get up off the guy he'd cuffed and pulled out his badge to identify himself to the local police.

She used the back of her sleeve to wipe her mouth. "Fine."

Murdock approached. He reached his hand out to her. She stared up at him and was going to refuse his brother's help as she didn't reach for his hand right away and tried to maneuver up herself, but then she cringed. Murdock grabbed her hand and pulled her up slowly. She pressed against him, and he held her.

"You have a mean right hook, sweetheart."

"And a few dirty moves," Mitch added, and she glanced at them.

"A girl's gotta do what a girl's gotta do."

Murdock snorted low and looked a little angry.

"You could have been hurt badly, even killed."

"You should have waited," Mitch added.

"They would have gotten away."

They heard some yelling and then turned to see Mrs. Phillips banging the steering wheel and having a tantrum.

"So you were saying something about foul play?" Mitch asked her as he reached for her chin to look at the damage to her lip. She looked so sexy, and he noticed Murdock kept his hands on her hips as he stood pressed against her back, being supportive..

"So, we're going to go over what went down and try to figure out how you pieced this together," Mitch stated.

"You stupid bitch. You ruined everything. Everything," Mrs. Phillips yelled at Mia, and Mia stared at her as a police officer held her by her hands that were cuffed behind her back.

"Got a large envelope of cash in here and some files, too, Detective," one of the other police officers yelled to Mitch.

"And you ruined your daughter's life and your grandchildren's lives by killing your husband for money to buy antiques."

Mrs. Phillips growled, and the officer pulled her away to place her into the back of the patrol car.

"Despicable woman," Mia said through clenched teeth and then cringed as she pressed her fingers to her lips.

"Mia, once we wrap everything up here, we're going to have that drink."

"What?"

"You heard me, Mia." He stepped closer and ran his thumb along her chin. He leaned closer and kissed her temple then inhaled against her, trying to ease a concern he had for her safety by absorbing her scent. She shivered.

"You scared the hell out of me," he scolded as he looked down into her dark-blue eyes.

"It was fine, and I was fine." She then gasped and turned toward Murdock, who must have given her hips a squeeze.

"My brother is right. I wouldn't deny a direct order from him."

"Really?" she asked and then looked between them.

"We have a first aid kit over here, Detective," one of the local officers told them, interrupting them.

Mia pulled away and followed the officer. Mitch looked at Murdock, who just stared at Mia as she walked with the officer then looked over her shoulder at the two of them.

"Does Tiegen know about her, too?"

Mitch smiled and couldn't help but feel excited because even Murdock was attracted to her. They could make their fantasies become a reality with Mia.

"He sure as shit does. You keep an eye on our girl. I'll give Tiegen the heads-up about her, and we'll get this mess cleaned up."

"Our girl, huh?" Murdock asked, and he didn't look so sure. He actually looked a little worried as he watched Mia.

"She's going to answer to me for that little stunt she pulled not waiting for backup. Mark my words." He then walked over toward the van to help try to figure out exactly what Mia had done to finally put these men behind bars once and for all.

* * * *

Mia held the ice pack against her lip as the police officer asked her where else she was hurt. She told him nowhere because she didn't want him fussing over her. She said thanks, and he headed over to help the others. Murdock, Mitch's brother, stood next to her with his arms crossed in front of his large chest. He was tall, like six three or something, and very muscular. From the military-style haircut, and tight, long-sleeved shirt that showed off chest and ab muscles, he was in super shape. But it was his dark-blue eyes and that look of experience—or was it mystery or a lost look?—that caught her full attention.

He uncrossed his arms. "Turn around, let me see your back." He stepped closer.

She stepped back and hit the side of the patrol car.

"I saw how you landed and how difficult it was for you to get up." He held her gaze.

"I'm fine."

He gave her an annoyed expression, and she felt a bit guilty but also on guard. Who was this guy, and what was with the instant bodyguard mode?

She looked past him.

"I should head over and help Mitch."

She saw the news crew of a local television station come onto the scene. Photographers were taking pictures, and the reporter was asking questions.

"Mia." She heard Mitch call her name, and when she and Murdock looked, he was by the building that the van was parked in front of, with the door opened. He waved her over. "You have your gear?"

She nodded.

"Bring it," he yelled, and she moved from the car, cringing as she walked. Murdock stayed right next to her.

"You're hurt."

"I'll be fine, Murdock." She reached into her Jeep Cherokee, and as she bent, she tried to hide the pain she was in.

"Let me help you." Murdock reached for her bags holding her equipment. Then they closed the door and headed toward the building. She already had her camera out and ready.

"I don't have a detailed list of all the items stolen from all those houses, but I have a feeling a lot of this will match," Mitch said as she walked through the doorway and saw all the boxes and tables set up with jewelry, computers, antiques, and other items.

Murdock whistled.

"I think that drink just turned into dinner, my treat, Mia. You broke the case wide open," Mitch told her, and she couldn't help but to smile softly.

But then that insecure feeling hit her belly hard, and she went right to work, focusing on taking the pictures, securing the evidence, and making sure Mrs. Phillips and her crew of thieves didn't get away with all those robberies and her husband's murder.

Chapter 3

Detective R.J. Duncan stood by the body as the forensics team did their thing. He ran his hand along his jaw and looked at his partner, Mosley Lane.

"This is crazy. The same MO, the same positioning of the body, and now this? He's staging the crime scene. What is he after?"

"I don't know, R.J. I mean, yeah, things match, including the bloody high heel at the entrance to the woods and the ripped clothing, but five years? Why suddenly now, after so long?"

"Maybe he was waiting. Maybe he hasn't found what he was looking for. I don't know. We never figured out why he chose Wynona. Why he was there in the apartment waiting that night? How the hell did he get her out of the apartment, and why wasn't Mia taken and killed, too?" He stared at the bloody, beaten body of the victim. She had long brown hair, an athletic build, large breasts. She was a beautiful young woman, just like the other victims from similar cases. He thought of Mia, and it hit him. He felt sick. Scared.

"What? What are you thinking?"

"That night, when Mia's roommate was abducted, Mia was out later then she should have been. Her roommate, Wynona, had been out drinking. Initially it was believed that some guy she may have flirted with followed her home and got inside and abducted her. It was later that we realized she had gone to lie down in Mia's bed, not her own."

"You mean this guy could have really had his eye on Mia?"

R.J. pulled his bottom lip between his teeth. Just thinking about it made him sick and angry. She was so damn special. He wished their relationship had worked out, but she just couldn't let go and let him in all the way.

"We tried not to focus on that. Mia took it hard. She had a rough childhood and basically raised herself, worked her way through college, and even getting that apartment with Wynona." He looked back at the body.

"These two women, the two cases we had, have too many similarities to Wynona's death. I looked into the system and tried to find any other cases with similar circumstances and came up with three."

"And?"

"And they indicated the time of death in each of the cases where the women's bodies were found fall possibly near the anniversary date of Wynona's abduction and death."

"Fuck."

"Mosley, all four of these women have long brown hair, dark eyes, athletic figures, and are laid out in the same fashion."

"You think that he might try to find Mia?"

R.J. exhaled. "Fuck, I don't even want to consider it. I mean it would be reaching. She wouldn't be hard to find. She moved less than an hour from the city."

"You must have her information and contact number still."

R.J. took a few steps back and Mosley walked with him.

"R.J., what the fuck is going on? I've never seen you like this. You always are straight-faced and right in the midst of investigations so we can find the ones responsible. If this woman is in danger, then you need to contact her and make sure she's on guard."

"I don't want to scare her unnecessarily. There's isn't quite enough evidence, and contacting her after not speaking to her for the last couple of years will be strange."

"Buddy, what is it? She was part of the case when her friend was murdered. You'd be doing the right thing by warning her."

"Mosley, I was working that murder investigation. Mia was part of the search party and found her friend's body first."

"Jesus."

R.J. looked away. "It was traumatic for her in so many ways. It took months for her to get rid of the nightmares. I don't think she ever really recovered."

"You didn't keep in touch with her to make sure she was okay?"

"We spent a lot of time together. She was trying to finish college and was all gung ho about being involved with forensics and photography."

"Wait, were you romantically involved with her?"

R.J. didn't answer.

"Oh damn, she's the one that got away. The one you've compared every woman you meet to, isn't she?" Mosley asked.

R.J. looked away and spoke toward the woods. "I know I need to call her. It's just that things ended badly. I hurt her. I walked away when she pushed me away. I went back on my promise to not be another person who left her behind and walked out of her life like her parents had, as had every other person she'd ever met."

"It's been five years since the murder and a few years since your relationship. Maybe she's involved with someone or married?"

He shook his head. "She lives alone in an apartment in Portland Place. She's a forensics photographer for the CI unit. She probably would have gotten called in on this investigation tonight but was caught up in another case in Yarland. I thought for sure I would see her and that she would probably make the same connections."

"If this guy is this close, leaving a body here and then two towns over and in the city, then he may already know where Mia is and be waiting to strike."

That got R.J.'s attention right away.

"I'll call her, make plans to meet in person. I'll give her the heads-up."

"I'll go with you if you want, unless your plan is to rekindle an old romance with her."

R.J. thought about that a moment. She'd given him her virginity, but even after that, after taking the chance they had with the huge difference in their ages, she'd never gave him her heart. That was what he wanted from her, but she just couldn't let her guard down long enough to give it to him.

* * * *

Mia didn't want to be here. She didn't want to spend time alone with Mitch and Murdock. They were too intense. They oozed control, power, and it affected her, almost making her feel weak. She'd never felt that way around any man. Not even R.J., who she'd given her virginity to.

She took an unsteady breath. Then she kept wringing her fingers over the steering wheel, gripped the steering wheel as she drove her Jeep along the road then into the parking lot of Crossroads. It wasn't helping that she had to drive Murdock back with her while Mitch took a ride with the other detectives in order to go over everything with them. She inhaled, liking the man's cologne. She liked how he looked in her Jeep. Or maybe it was the just the idea of not traveling back to Wellington alone that she liked.

She didn't know why she was thinking about R.J., about sex, and about getting close to a man. So what that Mitch and even Murdock flirted with her? It didn't mean a thing. She'd been flirted with numerous times, but most men learned that she wasn't biting or interested.

She shifted in her seat.

"Whether you like it or not, I'm going to take a look at your back as soon as we get to Crossroads."

"I told you that I'm fine and just a bit sore."

"You had some good moves there. How long have you studied Tae Kwon Do?" he asked her, ignoring her response. Would he try to look anyway? How would his hands feel against her skin?

"What makes you think I have?" she countered as she pulled into a parking spot.

"Come on, Mia, I may be just some dumb soldier, but I know the difference between academy training self-defense and the fine art of martial arts training."

She put the car in park and then looked at him.

"I think I'm going to pass on drinks and dinner. I'm feeling more sore and tired. It was an emotional day."

"You wouldn't want to upset Mitch. He's got this thing about people obeying orders. Kind of like me." He leaned closer. She thought he might kiss her, and she pulled back, but only slightly. He did smell really good, and there was this pull, an attraction to him that she just couldn't seem to shake. The thing was she felt it for Mitch, too.

He pulled the keys from the ignition and gave her a wink. "I'll just hold on to these to ensure you don't try to run off." She felt her mouth drop open, and then the annoyance hit her belly. She went to get out of the Jeep quickly and felt the ache. She closed her eyes and slowed her pace.

"Murdock, give me my keys. You have no right to take them from me. You hardly even know me."

He put them in his front pocket and kept his hand in there as he looked her over.

"They're safe with me. Now turn around and let me look at your back."

She crossed her arms in front of her chest and cringed again. Son of a bitch. She knew she was bruised. He arched one of his eyebrows and gave her that look of his. It matched his brother Mitch's and meant he was serious, or else.

She looked around them and noticed there was no one else coming or going from Crossroads that would see him lift her shirt a little. But did she really want him to touch her? She'd known him only hours.

"Please turn around, Mia." Murdock, with his firm, deep tone of voice, towering over her at over six feet tall, was saying he wanted to ensure she was okay.

Her eyes widened, and she was surprised by his sincere, calm tone and the fact that he wasn't ordering her. Although him ordering her around seemed to affect her in ways she hadn't expected. Her pussy pulsed and leaked, and she suddenly wished for the sensation and connection of sex, being that close to another human being and letting go. She looked at Murdock's big arms and large form, and she knew she would feel safe and protected in his arms. She gulped and reprimanded herself for acting like a needy child instead of the independent woman she'd been forced to become who relied solely on herself and not on others or on the influence of emotions. She could do this. She could handle Murdock touching her. She just knew she could.

"You're such a nag. Fine, get it over with," she said, trying to be forceful and sound unaffected, but the last syllables came out in a whisper.

When she sensed him step closer, and then he reached down for the hem of her shirt and slowly lifted it up, she felt faint, tense, ready to jump out of her shoes.

The moment his fingers brushed over her skin, she looked over her shoulder.

"Fine, right?" she asked, but he was in a dead stare at her back, and then she felt his hand on her hip, his finger tracing something.

"Damn, Mia, I don't think your little vine of daisies is supposed to be red, black, and blue."

She was surprised by his tone and how his fingers felt like they traced her skin and then, the tattoo along her hip to her lower back. He was exploring. She liked how it felt.

His hands felt so good, so gentle against her hips.

"It's a beautiful tattoo. The way it trails from your hip bone all the way back to practically your ass."

As he said the words, his fingers moved from her hip bone to a little lower in the front of her at her groin. She gasped and tilted forward, only for him to trail his fingers back and over the tattoo then to her ass, past where the tattoo stopped. He gave her ass a little tap.

"You are in tiptop shape, baby."

She went to push her shirt down, and he stopped her.

"One minute." He leaned down lower, and the next thing she felt, his hands still on her waist, was his lips touching her skin and then licking along the tattoo.

She closed her eyes and held her breath. "Murdock," she whispered in what she wanted to be a reprimanding tone but came out in a moan.

When he stood up, he pressed his front to her back and then whispered next to her ear.

"Let's head inside before I do something crazy." He then took her hand and led her from the car to the sidewalk. She walked with not only an ache in her back and her lips but also one in her pussy.

* * * *

Tiegen watched Mia as she stood near the crowd with their friends and some people Mia knew from work. She looked uncomfortable, never mind quiet, as she barely contributed to the conversation. He noticed Reed, one of the other forensic technicians, standing close to her and whispering to her. She kept moving away from him, and then Mitch stepped closer to Mia, placed his hand on her waist, and whispered into her ear. She didn't pull away. His brother's public show of possession wasn't missed by anyone, including Murdock.

"What do you know about her aside from her profession?" Murdock asked, joining Tiegen by the bar and sitting on one of the stools.

He glanced back at Mitch and saw him and Mia talking to one another as the crowd dispersed toward the pool tables.

"Nothing really. She's got a great reputation with her job. She knows a lot of people, and they respect her, but she's not very social."

Murdock looked back toward them. "I got that impression. She looks uncomfortable in crowds."

"Here they come," Tiegen said, and then Mitch pulled over another stool, bringing it closer to Tiegen so Mia could sit down. He stood behind her as Murdock ordered another round of beers.

"I'm good. I should probably get going." Mia clasped her hands in front of her and lowered her eyes. She was shy, yet from what his brothers had told him about her actions today, she was resourceful, quick, and tough as nails when she countered three men, taking them on by herself.

Mitch pressed up against her back and wrapped his arm around her waist. Tiegen noticed Mia tighten up, gasp, and place her hands over his forearm.

"Don't go. Stay, so my brothers and I can get to know you better," he whispered next to her hair.

"Mitch, this isn't a good idea," she replied.

Murdock crossed his arms in front of his chest and held her gaze, eyes squinted slightly.

"What's your deal?" he asked.

She straightened her shoulders. "My deal?"

"Yeah, you act shy and inexperienced around men, around us, yet in the heat of danger you're like a fearless superwoman. What gives, Mia?"

She stared at Murdock and then glanced at Tiegen, and Tiegen waited not so patiently for her response. He wanted to touch her, hold her like Mitch was doing, especially seeing her with that bruised cheek and split lip. He felt compelled to hold her and make any discomfort go away.

"Listen, I don't know what you guys are used to, but being manhandled, pulled around, and put on the defensive is not my thing." She went to push Mitch's arm off of her waist and midsection, but he didn't budge.

"Whoa, slow down. No one is manhandling you. I like you. We want to get to know you better," Mitch said to her.

She turned around in his arms.

"Why? What for? What do you want? Sex? A fling? I'm not interested. This is a waste of time. I don't date."

"I'm not interested in a fling. I'm interested in getting to know you." Mitch reached up and pressed his palm to her cheek. He stared at her lip.

"I'd kiss you right now and show you that these feelings are real, but your lip looks so sore." He leaned closer as if he were going to kiss her lips gently anyway, or maybe her cheek, when Mia turned away and grabbed onto his shoulders. She lowered her head.

"It will never work. I don't date. I'll just make you angry because I'll never open up or be what you want. I know how these relationships work, and we'll only get hurt. I need to go."

She pulled away and headed away from them. Mitch placed his hands on his hips and stared at her leaving. Tiegen crossed his arms in front of his chest.

Murdock grabbed his beer. "She's got a past," he said very calmly.

"She's been hurt before." Mitch ran his fingers through his hair.

"A guy?" Tiegen said.

"Definitely," Murdock added.

"It's more than that. Don't ask me how I know, but since I met her, watched her do her job, I've caught things. Different things, like when she was with those kids whose grandfather murdered. There was this look in her eyes, and it made me think that she knew how they felt, whether that meant their fear or their loss."

"She closes up when it's one-on-one and personal. But I saw her today in that dangerous situation, and it was like she had no fear whatsoever. I know that look, that type of action. It comes when you've witnessed violence and death often, and maybe experienced surviving when others around you die. It's like you're numb to things and fearless for your own safety." Murdock had this lost look in his eyes. Perhaps he was right. He would know as a soldier who'd witnessed everything he'd just said and then some. Death, surviving, not wanting to make a connection.

"Well, I don't know about you guys, but that just makes me want to know more about her. Makes me want to interrogate her and then demand she let down her guard and let us in. You two feel the connection, that attraction to her like I do, don't you?" Mitch asked, and Tiegen nodded.

"Maybe it's a waste of time." Murdock downed the rest of his beer before placing the empty bottle down on the bar.

They were quiet for a while.

"Mitch, you said that Mia spoke with Jethro before she went to see those kids and the mom. He's her boss but maybe he knows her on a personal level? He had to have done a thorough background check on her before accepting her into the position she has. They don't just hire anyone to be forensic photographers and enter crime scenes, and she definitely has a knack for more."

"Maybe you're right. Maybe Jethro can shine some light on what's going on here. But either way, I'm not going to let this go. She felt so good in my arms, and I love being close to her. This isn't over," Mitch said to them.

Chapter 4

He couldn't contain the excitement he felt. He almost didn't turn on the TV. He hated watching it, but the news was so helpful, indicating how close the police were in solving crimes and also in giving him ideas of what he would do to Mia when she was his woman. Every day there were stories of murder, rape, and violence. In fact, he was able to pull up the news reports from all over the United States if he wanted to. But that wasn't his interest.

When he saw Detective R.J. Duncan, he smiled from ear to ear. He didn't deserve Mia. He'd taken advantage of her youth, her innocence with his older, dominant ways. He slammed his fist into his palm and rotated it as he clenched his teeth. R.J. would die, but first he would put R.J. through hell. He'd failed Mia in so many ways. He failed to get her to become his fully because Mia belonged to him, not R.J., not any other man. He saw her first. Watched her since her first day of college and knew she was the one. She was so much like Colleen.

He closed his eyes and inhaled then exhaled, trying to calm his anger down. He'd lost it back then, wanted so much from Colleen, but she wasn't right in the end. Adopted, a woman without a family, and he wanted to be her everything. He eased his way into her life, and they became lovers so quickly his head spun. But soon he saw the things she was lacking and knew she wasn't exactly what he wanted. Plus, she began to pull back and started talking about seeing other people. He was the man, the one in charge, and he would say when the relationship was over. He'd taken her virginity, and he owned her completely, so when she tried to leave, he didn't let her, and he ended her life because he had that right, that power, because Colleen belonged to him.

He took a deep breath and then exhaled as he leaned back into the old plaid recliner. He closed his eyes, and he saw them. Like he did every night in his dreams, his nightmares, he saw them. The women he hunted over the years, the ones he captured and killed in order to try to get Colleen out of his head and train in preparation for the day Mia was in his arms and his possession. They all looked the same. Same hair color, same bodies, same eyes, and same innocence. But it was never enough, and the police were getting closer, so he had to pull back and regroup. He had to try to figure out who could replace Colleen forever. That was the first time he'd seen her. Mia. She lived in the same apartment building. He knew her parents had been old and died, leaving her to fend for herself. Then that jerk tried to get her in his car, and he knew he had to do something. He intervened. He thought that was it. That she was too young. But each time he saw Mia after that, and watched her blossom in a year's time, seeking her out whenever she was nearby, he knew he was growing fond of her. In his head, he gradually began to no longer look for women who reminded him of Colleen. He began to look for women who reminded him of Mia.

Then one day she moved out, all while he was entertaining a kill and disposing of the body. In that long weekend, she disappeared.

He swallowed hard remembering the sudden shock to his system as he watched the young couple with a baby move into Mia's old place. His heart grew heavier and heavier each day. He saw her in all things and all places. A woman with brown hair getting onto a bus. He ran quickly to catch up, and when the woman turned, she wasn't Mia.

He drew her picture, searched the Internet, asked the neighbors questions, and then he heard she might have gone to the local university. Weeks passed, then months, until he finally couldn't get her out of his head so he went to all the places co-eds hung out. The campus, the local bars, the community workout center.

He started buying things for her, planning when they would be together and deciding that she would be the final one. That he would spend the rest of his life loving her, having her body, and making her all he ever wanted. No one else in the world mattered. But his obsession turned into such need and desire he was becoming desperate to act out his fantasies and prepare for the day Mia was his.

As he sat in the little café and deli near campus, he searched for the right woman, the one to practice on. He grew inpatient until he saw her, standing in line at the café down the street from the community college.

Her long brown hair, slim-fitting skirt, conservative top, and perfectly round ass grabbed his attention. His cock instantly hardened, and he knew she would do even before she turned. This woman was mature, sexy, voluptuous, and more than likely not a student at the college. He had to see her face, and when she turned and he saw her smile, her angelic expression, he nearly took her right there. Mia. *My Mia.*

She was beyond beautiful, and sexy, too. Her breasts bigger than Colleen's, her body made to please a man and then some. No longer a maturing woman but a fully blossomed goddess. She was all woman, yet she was shy, reserved, and virgin-like. That part of her personality had appealed to him two years before. It was part of why he searched for others like her and always came up short. There was no one like Mia. His obsession with Colleen and finding ones like her had been a waste of time because, right here before him, stood destiny.

He licked his lips and could practically taste her scent, her perfume, and feel her sweetness. He moved closer to her, close enough to know her perfume and to know that her eyes were of the darkest blue he had ever seen. Those eyes would glisten with love for him, with passion and lust as he sank his cock deep into her depths and made her his forever.

His plan was foolproof, or so he thought. He had everything set up in the cottage in the woods. The drive was a good hour away from the city but the place was perfect for seducing his woman and making her scream and beg for him to fuck her over and over again.

The sound of the television and a commercial with sirens and alarms brought him back to the present. He felt his whole body tense and shake with need. He needed inside of her. He needed to take from her body, and he needed it now.

He was breathing heavily. His cock was hard within his jeans, and he knew he wouldn't be able to hold off much longer. He had to find her. He was getting so close. But back then, he'd fucked up somehow. He was so obsessed, so impatient, that he grabbed her roommate instead of Mia. He'd fucked up, and the only thing to do was to get rid of her. Wynona had been a slut, and she always tried to get Mia to go to bars with her and to pick up men, but Mia always left. She never stuck around past eleven. She was a good girl, and she was waiting for him to claim his woman. Wynona suffered the consequences of trying to taint Mia. But in punishing her, torturing her, and killing Wynona, it cost him everything. Mia had fallen into the arms of R.J. Duncan.

He had to hide and lay low. He knew he'd fucked up, but he needed time. Time to recoup and to train and prepare himself to be patient and calm with Mia or he could wind up killing her, too. Knowing she was fucking another man just made him realize how much more he could do with her sexually and more quickly than if she were a virgin. So he set to work on a plan, a means to get what he wanted, and Mia disappeared.

In the last five years, he'd decided to practice, to prepare for her to be his woman, his wife, his everything. But then he had the urge and the need to kill again, to grab a woman who reminded him somewhat of Mia and take from her, practice on her what he wanted to do to Mia, but things got out of hand. He was getting better, but then when

R.J. turned up to be the detective investigating the homicides, his revenge began to build a new plan.

R.J. would pick up on the details, the evidence left behind, and he would know that it was him, the same man, the killer who'd taken Wynona's life when he meant to take Mia's. When he finally had Mia, there would be nothing R.J. could do. He would know that Mia truly belonged to him and not R.J., and the suffering and pain would send R.J. into a state of fear and panic. But he wouldn't find him and Mia, no one would, and the two of them would disappear into the woods to live out his fantasies and hers together.

He glanced at the television as thoughts of finding Mia filled his heart and his mind. He was getting closer, especially living right outside of the city. R.J. would lead him to her. He just knew it.

He heard the report, something about home invasions and a man being killed and how local Portland Place detectives and a forensic photographer had broken the case. He had to do a double take. He clicked the record button on the remote as he thought he saw her. Then the camera scanned the police cruisers and vehicles again as men were handcuffed and arrested.

"Mia." He saw her standing by two men, her lip bleeding, holding an ice pack against her cheek but looking even more beautiful than ever before.

"I found you. My God, I found you."

He could barely contain his excitement and catch his breath his heart was beating so rapidly.

He looked at everything and listened to all they were saying. She was thirty minutes away. She was a hero in solving that case, and she would be his sooner than he ever expected.

He jumped up and looked around the room. There was so much to do. He'd thought he had more time, but this proved she was meant to be his. He almost didn't turn on the television. *My God, Mia is so close. I can get to her. I can have the life I always wanted with her. I need to get the cabin fully stocked. I need to grab everything we'll need for months, for years, to live up there.* The snow would be falling sooner than later. By November there'd be inches, if not feet, up in the mountains. He had to plan this right. He had to make it so no one would be able to track them or follow and do any search and rescue missions.

Patience, Peter. Patience. There's no need to rush this. I have plenty of time, and this is what I have been training for. He closed his eyes and took a deep breath, feeling as if he could smell her scent. *Mine. Mia is finally going to be all mine.*

* * * *

Mia was going over some paperwork at her desk when Reed walked over. He sat down in the chair next to her and smiled.

"What's up?" he asked.

"Just doing a bunch of paperwork."

"I bet it's a lot considering your involvement in that home invasion case. Pretty cool stuff." He gave her arm a nudge.

She gave a small smirk but kept working.

"It was good to see you out at Crossroads. I don't think I've ever seen you out anywhere."

"When is there time to go out? We've been pretty busy for months."

"Yeah, kind of sucks that we are. It means the world is full of evil people."

"It sure is, but it's not as bad as all that. We're busy because what we do is so time consuming and there isn't room for mistakes."

"That's true. So, question for you. What made you go out to Crossroads?"

She turned to look at him and felt a bit uncomfortable. She talked to her coworkers but mostly kept to herself.

"I had to give the detective's brother a ride back to Wellington. They were planning on meeting some friends, and I got roped into a few drinks."

"Looked like you weren't minding their company."

"Reed, what do you want? I'm trying to get through all this stuff and then head out to town for some things this afternoon."

"Just wanted to know if you wanted to maybe go out for coffee sometime, or some drinks, dinner? Maybe?"

She swallowed hard. "I don't think so. I don't date. I don't like going out that much."

"Why not?"

"I just don't, okay? I'm sorry. I don't want to get involved with anyone, especially someone I work with. Friends, okay?" she said to him, firmly but nicely.

He smiled. "Okay. For now. But I won't give up hope unless you are seeing someone else. Or maybe three someones?" he teased and then stood up. She felt her cheeks warm, and he winked.

"I don't really know the McKay brothers, just Mitch sort of, but from what I saw last night, they have their eyes on you, and they're older, pretty intense men. Mitch always gets what he wants and is known as a pit bull in the field of homicide investigation."

"That's nice to know, but I'm not interested. I don't even know them."

He shrugged. "Just saying it was good to see you out in the social world, and if he had something to do with that, it's cool."

He walked away, and Mia tried to start typing again but couldn't. She instantly thought about Mitch, Tiegen, and Murdock. She actually hadn't minded at all going out to Crossroads. In fact, a couple of the women in the lab had asked her to join them for a drink tomorrow night. Then, of course, others joined in saying they would meet there. No one from the labs or the coroner's office went out like that. They were all workaholics, or so she'd thought. It was hard to say no, and she didn't know why she said yes when she hated coming home alone at night to an empty apartment. But she had. She'd said she would and now she might have to deal with seeing Reed, who obviously liked her. She hoped he got her message that she wanted to be friends. She could do friends but nothing more.

She sighed. It was crazy, but she was entirely too attracted to Mitch, Tiegen, and Murdock. Yet, Murdock and Tiegen held back a bit and acted so distant, even when they flirted a little. Mitch was forward, almost commanding in the sense that he didn't hesitate touching her and pulling her close. Though it made her tense and freak out slightly, she had to admit that it felt good. But maybe just being hugged like that was what she was holding on to. When she thought about it, it had been years since she was hugged, truly held and cared for by anyone.

That was pretty fucking lame. She felt the tears sting her eyes. Actual tears. What the hell was going on?

She felt guilty, as though she had been mean to them before she left. She'd walked away when Mitch was telling her how they wanted to get to know her. Three men, brothers, wanted to be close to her and get to know her. Everything about that scared her. The conversation, the being held, the flirting, the intimacy of a man's touch. Times that by three and, holy shit, she was scared out of her mind. But she wasn't stupid. She knew what really had her confused. She'd never thought about having a relationship with a man again. Not after R.J. and how things had gone wrong. She wasn't capable of fully trusting anyone. She wasn't able to let down her guard and let go and be free. She just couldn't do it. She'd conditioned herself to be independent and never rely on anyone but herself.

She had no family, no ties to anything. The only reason she lived in Portland Place was because, after college and with the help of her professor who thought she was super talented, she'd wound up getting a job nearby. She hated her apartment, she hated the city, and she disliked feeling unconnected, yet she'd embraced it and become so attached and reliant on it that it had hardened her and made her more alone than ever before.

She looked at the computer screen and refocused on her work. She needed to clear her mind. She thought about what Reed had said, about her never going out and how she'd looked as though she was having fun. For a moment that thought made her feel normal, when most of her life she'd felt so abnormal. Perhaps going out with Amy and Alyssa would be a good thing. How could it hurt to make a few friends? It wasn't as if she wanted or needed companionship. She wasn't good at it anyway. If she didn't go and the rest of the office went, then she would really stand out as the oddball. She sighed. *I'll just decide after work. If I drive there, then the decision is made for me.*

She finished up the report and then added it to the e-mail, printed a copy out, and then added it to the thumb drive as backup before looking at the clock. Lunchtime. She needed some fresh air, despite how windy it seemed to be out there. She grabbed her purse and her sweater plus the crocheted hat that matched and headed toward the stairs.

When she got outside, she walked through the lobby and watched people holding their jackets tightly as leaves danced around. It was pretty darn windy, but the little café and luncheonette was around the corner.

She pulled her hat onto her head, grateful for the warmth and also loving how designer it looked with her long brown hair and matching the wool sweater wrapped her body. The wind blew in gusts and then dissipated before repeating the same gusts a little harder as she made her way down the block.

The moment she rounded the corner, she saw the line for the luncheonette and cringed. Too long. She passed by knowing that another two blocks up and a bit out of the way was a local pizza place that had a small deli and salad bar. A lot of cops went there for coffee and lunch. It was fast and convenient. She figured she could grab a salad to go if necessary if there weren't any seats left.

As she headed that way, a gust of wind blew her hat off, and she gasped as her hair whipped over her face, stopping her from turning to grab her hat. A moment later, as she turned, she spotted Tiegen and another guy.

She pushed her hair from her face as he approached. "Lose something?" he asked.

She reached for the hat and held his gaze when she looked up into his eyes.

"Thank you."

"Damn, Tiegen, you tore that hat from my hands," the guy with him said, and it was obvious he was flirting as he looked her over and gave her a wink.

"Gus, meet Mia," Tiegen told his friend, never taking his eyes off of her.

"Damn." Gus shook his head. "Nice to meet you, Mia."

Mia looked at Gus, who had his hand out, and she shook it. As the wind blew again, Gus started walking, and the wind was so strong Mia nearly lost her balance.

Immediately Tiegen wrapped his arm around her waist and pulled her close.

"This wind is wild. You need some help?"

Her hair whipped in front of her, and Tiegen reached up and caressed it behind her ear. He then placed his palm against her cheek as she held on to his forearms. "I'm good."

He smiled. "You heading inside?"

She nodded.

"Join me then."

"What about Gus?"

"He'll fend for himself. We met up a block the other way. Come on."

He guided her along the rest of the way, keeping a hand at her waist and around her. When they entered the place, she saw some familiar faces and immediately people started waving to Tiegen. He placed his hands on her shoulders as they walked.

He gave a few smiles and nods, but that was it as he squeezed her shoulders. He seemed to be acting protective of her.

"It's crowded," he whispered next to her ear.

"Sure is. But the café near the office is worse. The line was out the door."

Someone behind the counter asked who was next. Before long, it was their turn to order, and she got a chicken Caesar salad, and Tiegen got the cheese steak sandwich with salad.

As they looked around for a spot to sit, someone waved at Tiegen.

"Come on," he told her, and she followed, even though the small table for two was taken by two men in suits.

"Hey, Tiegen, what's going on?" one of the guys asked.

"Just grabbing a quick lunch."

"Well, take this table. We're all done. Got a call for a job."

"Shit. Good luck."

"Yeah, you too." The guy winked as he looked at Mia. The other one looked at her, too.

"This is Mike and Clay. Guys, this is Mia."

They nodded and then headed away.

Mia went to take the seat that would keep her back against the wall and her eyes on the doorway, but Tiegen stopped her.

"Let me sit there."

She swallowed hard.

"I've got your back, baby. Don't you worry," he said as if he knew why she wanted to sit there. Was it a cop thing? A means to be on guard all the time for Tiegen? Because for her, it ensured no surprises and was a similar reason. She took the seat as the uneasy feeling filled her chest.

He reached over and covered her hand.

"Trust me."

"I'm fine," she snapped at him, and he eased his hand back and started eating.

"Slow day at the office?" he asked her in between bites.

She took a few bites of her salad. "Not really. A lot of paperwork."

"From yesterday's events?"

"Yes."

"Well, you did great. So what else do you do with the department?"

"You mean besides photographing dead bodies and collecting evidence at crime scenes?"

He chuckled. "Yep."

"Process the photos, try to find links, and even a little profiling if I can."

"Is that part of the job description?"

"Nope. Jethro and the department have me doing a lot of things. There's no real specific job description. Believe me, they keep me busy."

"So why forensic photography and forensics?" he asked, and she put her fork down and wiped her mouth before taking a sip of ice tea.

She didn't know how to answer that question.

"Mia?"

She released a breath. "I guess I have a knack for it. I took some classes in college and then did photography on the side and, well, combined the two. With support and training from one of my college professors, I wound up in forensics and working with Jethro."

"He has a lot of positive things to say about you."

She took another bite of salad. "You know Jethro well?"

"Unfortunately, in my profession, I have to meet with him often."

"Mitch too, I'm sure."

"Yes, he knows us both. In fact, I bet he would vouch for us if you wanted to take us up on that dinner date and drinks."

She felt her cheeks warm as she placed the fork down and then took a sip from her tea. "Tiegen."

"Tell me that you haven't thought about my brothers and me," he said to her in a low voice.

She pulled her lower lip between her teeth and then lowered her eyes. He reached over and placed his fingers under her chin, tilting it up toward him. Their gazes locked, and she felt her body hum with an awareness and an instant attraction to Tiegen. He was tall, muscular, and good-looking, even with the scruff along his chin and cheeks. It made him appear rugged, a little wild and hard, and it aroused her senses.

"Tell me you feel nothing, even right now with me this close, touching your skin and holding your gaze."

She was trying to speak but couldn't.

"I don't know what you're afraid of. I don't know if it's the whole ménage thing or some bad past experience with a man or men, but meeting like this, feeling this attraction like my brothers and I haven't felt before, just can't be ignored."

"Tiegen, please."

He brushed his thumb along her lips, and she so badly wondered what it would be like to get kissed by him. By Murdock and Mitch, too. Her cheeks immediately warmed again, and she knew she was blushing.

He released her chin and smiled. "Good. I can handle shyness. We'll work it out, even if going slow is torture."

She didn't know what to say. They finished their lunch and spoke about the upcoming Halloween events going on in Portland Place and Wellington at Crossroads.

"You planning on attending the event at Crossroads? The grand prize for best costume is five hundred dollars."

"Not my thing. How about you guys?"

"We'll go probably to support some of our crazy friends."

She smiled. "What are some of them going as?"

They talked some more, and she started getting more and more comfortable with him. She was wondering if maybe she could be friends with Tiegen and his brothers and nothing more. That thought brought an ache to her heart, and she realized she already liked them more than that. She needed to get out of here.

"Well, I should get back. I have so much to do. Thanks for saving my hat." She stood up.

"You sure you need to go?"

"Yes, Tiegen."

He pulled together his stuff and prepared to leave with her. "I'll walk you back."

"You don't need to."

"You may need hat rescuing again," he teased as they headed out the door.

She grinned. "Seriously?" she asked as he placed his hand at her lower back, guiding her onto the windy sidewalk.

She chuckled as they headed out and then heard her cell phone ringing.

She reached into her bag as they walked and saw a number she didn't recognize. "Hello?"

"Hi, Mia. It's R.J."

Mia stopped walking, and Tiegen looked at her with a concerned expression.

R.J. said her name again. "Mia?"

"Hold on a moment, R.J." She looked at Tiegen. "Thanks, but I need to take this call."

"No problem. See you soon," he said, but he looked hurt, maybe suspicious or even jealous.

She didn't have time to analyze his expression as she took a deep breath and started walking the rest of the way alone.

"Sorry, I was just finishing up with a friend at lunch."

"Can you talk?"

"Sure, I'm walking back to the office."

"How are you, sweetie?" he asked, and she felt the tears hit her eyes. His voice sounded so deep, so masculine, and yet also tired. She hadn't heard from him in so long. She wondered why he'd called now. What could he possible want to talk to her about?

"I'm good. Working a lot. How about you? Still doing the job in the city?"

"Of course. You know it's my life."

"I know," she replied, remembering trying to partly blame the downfall of their relationship on him, the hours he worked, and how they crossed paths in the night or in the early morning hours. That wasn't a schedule to keep as a couple. But ultimately it had been her that caused the breakup.

"I wanted to come see you in person. There are some things going on with these cases I've been involved in for the last year. I'm swamped."

"Do you need something from me?" she asked and then heard her phone buzz and then ring.

"Wait, hold on a moment. It's work calling me." She placed him on hold and got the message. There was a homicide, and she needed to get back to the office and grab her gear.

"I'm so sorry, R.J., but there's a homicide, and I need to photograph."

"I'll call you later or tomorrow or something."

"Okay. Bye." She disconnected the call and then hurried down the street. She couldn't help but wonder what had possessed R.J. to call her. Then it hit her. Something about a case he was working on. He wanted to talk to her in person. Could he have found Wynona's killer? Or be getting close? She'd thought the case was cold.

Her heart pounded, but the moment she got back into the office and began to grab her gear as the team gathered their own stuff, she no longer focused on R.J. or her nice lunch with Tiegen. She focused on her job and ensuring that everything was done right the first time to catch the person responsible for the crime.

* * * *

"You need a beer?" Murdock asked Mitch as he arrived at Crossroads.

"Yeah, thanks. Where's Tiegen?"

"He should be coming along soon. How was your hike through the woods?"

"It was great. I got back a couple of hours ago, showered, rested a bit."

Mitch smiled. "You hang out at the spot?"

"What do you think?"

Mitch shook his head and smiled. "Damn, I wish I could take some time off and go there, you know camp out before it gets too damn cold with the snow and shit."

"Too damn cold? What are you, a fucking pussy? We used to lay out there in the tents with the special gear during a damn blizzard."

"Well, it's been years."

They were quiet for a moment. "We should consider going again. Maybe next weekend or something?"

"Do a little hunting, too?"

"I get to hunt all the time in my job. I'll pass and concentrate on just getting away from it all," Murdock said.

"I get to hunt, too, with my job. The best feeling is to close a case and catch a killer." He took a sip from his bottle of Bud.

"Speaking of closed cases, Tiegen see Mia again after the other day at lunch?"

"I don't think so. He didn't really want to talk about what happened."

"Maybe he'll share over a few beers tonight?" Murdock said, and Mitch nodded.

"Maybe."

* * * *

"Oh God, I didn't think we were going to make it here tonight. Not after the last few days," Amy said as she, Alyssa, and Mia headed from the parking lot to the entrance of Crossroads. A few other people were headed inside, and as they made it to the sidewalk, Mia spotted Tiegen.

"Hello, Detective McKay," Alyssa said, flirting, and Tiegen gave a nod. Mia watched him and instantly felt that hint of jealousy that the two women liked Tiegen and flirted so shamelessly.

"Mia," he said, and Amy looked at Mia and smiled then grabbed Alyssa's arm.

"We'll meet you inside, Mia," Amy said, and Mia heard Alyssa say "lucky girl" as they headed inside.

Tiegen crossed his arms in front of his chest, and she stared up into his dark-brown eyes. His expression was firm, and his jaw was, too, and she could see the tiny veins by the side of his temple pulsating. He seemed angry.

"How are you doing?" he asked her.

"I'm doing good, and you?"

He didn't respond. He stepped closer. "I enjoyed spending lunch with you the other day."

"Me too." She felt her breasts tingle and her thighs felt funny, too, as though she was shaking in her heels or something. He stepped closer.

"Really? Because you kind of blew me off when you got that phone call." She was shocked at his tone and the fact that he seemed angry about the call and she wondered why. She was no good at understanding men who had an interest in her other than friendship.

"What do you mean?"

He uncrossed his arms and placed his hands on her hips. She held on to his forearms.

"Who is R.J. and is it serious?" he asked.

"Tiegen." She looked away, and he pulled her into his arms snugly. He cupped her cheek and chin, tilting it up toward him. He looked so sexy, so fierce and serious. She shivered with desire, and it shocked her.

"Tell me the truth. Is he a boyfriend?"

"No."

"Is he why you won't accept us?" he asked, shocking her, and she'd parted her lips to speak when he growled low. "Fuck it." He pressed his lips to hers and kissed her.

Mia held on to him. She was shocked by his moves, by the emotions she felt and the powerful desires that filled her heart and her body. She kissed him back, never feeling so much desire for a man while he kissed her. She felt his hand move from her lower back to her ass, and he squeezed her ass and devoured her moans.

It wasn't until she heard someone call out "get a room" that she realized they had caused a scene.

Tiegen released her lips and took her hand. "Come with me now," he said low, his voice deep and sexy.

He pulled her through the parking lot to his truck. It was parked by the end, in the dark, and he brought her around to the side, not giving her a moment to process what was happening when he pulled her close and kissed her once again.

It was passionate, wild, hot, and she ran her fingers through his brown hair and felt the strong muscles in his shoulders, and then his hands massaged up under her skirt to her ass. The fact that his fingers and the cool air of the night hit the crack of her ass at the same time brought her back to the present. She pulled from his lips.

"Tiegen, slow down."

But he continued to kiss her skin, her neck, and shoulder. He used his hands to knead the flesh of her ass and thighs. She absorbed the scent of his cologne and the feeling of his lips pressed against her skin and his muscles on his chest. She couldn't stop caressing him, and he couldn't stop tasting her.

"I'm going to tell you something right now. This is amazing, baby. This is not something to take lightly. I hope you realize that." He gripped her hips and gave her a shake. He held her gaze as she stared up into his eyes and continued caressing his shoulders and chest.

"I want you. I want to get lost inside this sexy body and see where this leads."

"Tiegen, God, this is crazy. It won't work."

"We want you, too."

She gasped and turned to see Murdock and Mitch standing there.

Tiegen hadn't blinked an eye. Was she so lost in Tiegen's kiss and words that she'd lost all sense of being safe and keeping an eye on what was going on around her?

"How did you—"

"Heard our brother snagged a hot, sexy woman around the waist and was practically mauling her in the parking lot," Murdock teased, and Tiegen pressed her against the truck.

"I think Mia was doing a little mauling herself." He covered her mouth and kissed her again. She was on fire with desire.

Then she felt him pull back as he continued to kiss her, pulling up her skirt and massaging her ass. As he turned, she felt the hands on her ass, Tiegen's hands, move down and then Mitch whispered against her ear.

"You have a great ass, Mia. I can't wait to explore it with my lips, my tongue, and my cock." He squeezed her ass, and she felt her pussy cream.

Mitch cleared his throat. "I think maybe we need to take this somewhere more private."

Tiegen slowly released her lips while Murdock fixed her skirt. As she tried to speak, her emotions got the better of her, and then Murdock turned her around and kissed her next. She was shocked. Well, shocked was too modest of a term here. She felt the same intense, wild desire and attraction to Murdock as she did for Tiegen.

In fact, she felt herself let go a bit and enjoy the kiss. She found herself thinking about how it would feel to have Mitch kiss her, too, and be surrounded by such big men with large muscles and even larger personalities. They were taking charge of this moment and of her body, too.

His hands moved over her hips and her ass then pressed her tightly to him. Murdock was super big and tall. So tall he had to lift her up and press her against the truck to bring them level to one another. When he slowly released her lips, he was breathing just as rapidly as she was.

"Damn, woman, you taste so good."

"Oh God, this is too much. The three of you are way too much to handle."

He slowly set her down, and Mitch took her hand and brought her to him. He cupped her cheeks and held her gaze as he stared down into her eyes. She held on to his hands and focused on his lips and then the need and hunger in his eyes.

"Baby, I think you can handle us, no problem at all." He covered her lips and kissed her, too, and she knew she was in trouble. There was no way she could walk away from them or push them away from her. No way at all.

Mitch slowly released her lips.

"Car keys?" Murdock asked her.

She looked around for her purse that was on the ground. Tiegen picked it up and licked his lower lip as he stared at her. The chill of the air didn't help to cool the heat of her body or her libido. Her sweater was opened, and her blouse undone slightly, revealing more cleavage than she would ever expose.

"Keys. Hand them over," Murdock said again with his palm out.

"Why?"

"Because you're coming home with us. We're going to explore these feelings we have and stop denying them. You'll come with me. Mitch will drive his truck, and Murdock will drive yours," Tiegen told her as he held her shoulder and neck and smiled softly down at her. He looked so sexy and desirable. She wanted him. She hadn't had sex in years, and here she was contemplating having sex with three men. That meant she would have to open up to them and let them in.

"I can't. I'm sorry. I just can't." She held her purse to her chest and backed up. Tiegen stopped her and held her close. "What's wrong? Why are you running from this?"

"Is it the sharing thing? So you what, never had a ménage before? Do we scare you?" Mitch asked her.

She shook her head. "I've never had sex with more than one man. I haven't had sex in a long time, and I don't sleep around."

"Of course you don't. It's one of the reasons you're so appealing. You're shy, modest, sweet, but also tough. There's a fighter in you, and we like that," Murdock told her.

"You're making this so difficult."

"Good," the three of them said together, and then she snorted low.

"No, not good. I hardly know the three of you. I don't date."

"Is it because of R.J.?" Tiegen asked, and she was shocked.

"What?"

"Who is R.J.?" Murdock asked, crossing his arms in front of his chest.

Mitch squinted at her. "You're seeing someone?"

"No. God, Tiegen, why are you bringing him up again?"

"Because I saw your face when he called the other day when we were walking after lunch. Everything stopped. It was like he came first."

She felt the chill in the air. Her body was losing the heat from their kisses and sensual touches, and now she was feeling cold and alone again. How did they have the power to make her feel safe and whole? It didn't matter anyway because here she was screwing things up before they even got started.

"I think I should head inside." She started to walk, and Tiegen grabbed her hand and pulled her close. He pressed her hand to his chest.

"Be honest. Don't lie. Are you seeing him?"

"No."

"Were you seeing him at some point?"

She swallowed hard. "Yes." She felt the tears hit her eyes.

"Do you still have feelings for him?" Mitch asked.

She looked at him and nodded. "I'll always have feelings for him. He was my first and only."

"Lover?" Murdock asked, sounding so shocked.

"Yes."

"No others?" Tiegen asked her as he cupped her cheek.

She tried turning away. "Do we need to discuss my inexperience right now?"

"Yes," Mitch said to her.

"Why?"

"Because it explains your fears."

"I'm not afraid," she snapped at him.

"Then come home with us tonight. Come see where this leads. Forget about R.J. or anything else and just let go with us."

She couldn't believe what he was saying and how she was considering accepting the offer. But what would it be like when things went wrong and when she hurt them and pushed them away or became cold, distant because she was too scared to let go?

"Say yes, Mia," Mitch said to her.

Murdock took her hand, which held her keys, brought it to his lips, and kissed her knuckles. "We want you. Let us in."

She felt the tears fill her eyes. "I don't know how," she whispered, and her voice cracked.

"We'll show you," Mitch said, and she looked at each of them and followed her gut and her heart. She nodded.

Mitch headed out, and so did Murdock. Tiegen unlocked the truck door and helped her get up and into the truck. She was shaking with a combination of fear and anticipation. She was going to do this. She was going to have sex with three men she was attracted to, and nothing else mattered. Then she felt the fear. It wouldn't work out. She would screw it all up, and this time, it would hurt three times as badly as the first time.

* * * *

Tiegen reached over to caress Mia's thigh, and she tightened up. A quick glance at her and he could tell she was scared. But his gut told him it was more than she was letting on. He and his brothers could be pretty demanding, especially in bed with a woman. He already knew this was going to be different. He already had such deep desires and feelings for Mia, and he hardly knew her. There was just something about her that pulled him toward her. But they weren't the type of men to coerce a woman to make love. Maybe comfort her, guide her if she were inexperienced, but not manipulate or force her. He had to find out why she was so scared to the point of shaking and sitting so far away.

"Mia?"

She swallowed hard.

"I want you to know that if you're not ready for this, if you're not feeling the attraction and desire, that it's okay. We can slow things down and take our time. We've got all the time in the world. You know that, don't you?"

She looked at him. "Really? You would stop right now and give me time?"

He took a deep breath and slowly released it as he stopped at the red traffic light. He looked at her. "It would kill me inside because I want you, want to explore your body, bring you pleasure and soak in every bit of you, but yes, I would, and so will Mitch and Murdock."

She nodded, and he could see the tears in her eyes. She leaned back. The light turned green, and he accelerated and gripped the wheel. He couldn't help but to hope she didn't want that, that she would open up and she would just give this a chance. But she was taking a risk. A woman who engaged in sex with multiple men at once was risking so much emotionally, physically, and it wasn't something to be forced but to desire.

"I love the way the three of you make me feel from a simple touch," she whispered, breaking the silence.

He pulled along the long road that led up to their private home in the heavily wooded area, parked the truck, turned off the ignition, pulled out the keys, and looked at her.

She turned to hold his gaze and her hand moved over the one he had pressed against the seat between them. So badly he wanted to close that space and draw her in close to kiss her, infuse faith into her that he and his brothers wouldn't hurt her.

"I'm scared, Tiegen. I'm scared for more reasons than I could get out or explain in such a short period of time."

"What do you mean a short period of time?"

"Tonight, in this moment, with Mitch and Murdock approaching the truck. It's a yes or no, a take a chance and live for tonight or not, but I know what tomorrow will bring."

He brought her fingers to his lips and kissed them. "It will bring more lovemaking, more pleasure and feeling complete in one another's arms."

She smiled softly, but it didn't reach her eyes. She wasn't happy. She was sad, and his gut clenched.

"You don't think this will last between us?"

"I know it won't."

His chest tightened, and he felt a bit angry at her saying such a thing, but then she added, "Because I'll ruin it. I'll push you away. I'll frustrate you because…I don't know how to love. I can't accept it. I can't open my heart to it."

"Why?"

"Too many reasons."

He looked toward her window and saw Mitch and Murdock standing there. Their expressions of concern were met with his stern expression and a nod to go ahead inside the house. They would get his drift, and when he had a moment, he would let them know to go slow with Mia and that whatever happened tonight depended on her.

"Why don't you come inside and see what happens? We want to be with you and to get to know you. We'll take our time."

She nodded and then opened the door. He got out and took a deep breath. *Who hurt her? Why is she so afraid? I want her. Please let her take a chance. Please.*

* * * *

Mitch knew something was up. One look from Tiegen and then Mia and he knew that they needed to put on the brakes and slow things down.

"Welcome to our home," Mitch told her, and she smiled.

"This is so big. My God, the ceilings are high."

She continued to compliment as she walked farther into the room, her heels clicking and clacking on the tile flooring. She looked so classy, sexy, and he wondered what she looked like naked. With thoughts of that came images of what it would feel like with her legs wrapped around his waist and his cock buried deep in her pussy. He wanted to hear her moan with pleasure, cry out his name, and give over all control to him, Tiegen, and Murdock.

There was an open floor plan, so from where she stood, she had a view of the large living room with floor-to-ceiling fireplace and the kitchen, as well as the stairs that led to a sunken den.

"We brought it from an architectural engineer Tiegen knew from the city. It had been his vacation home until he moved out to

California and bought a place in Colorado. We fixed it up, added our own designs," Mitch said to her.

"It's impressive. I don't think I've ever been in a home that looked like this. It's big."

Murdock took her hand and brought it to his lips. "We're big." He kissed her knuckles.

She shyly lowered her eyes, and Mitch saw Tiegen shake his head, as if saying to not push. Murdock saw him, too, as he looked up.

"How about a drink? We could sit in the living room or do a tour of the house?" Tiegen asked.

"A drink sounds nice." She clasped her hands in front of her.

Mitch watched her walk around, and they looked at some of the paintings and even a photograph taken by the lake.

"This is gorgeous. Is that by a local photographer?"

Mitch smiled. He placed his hand on her shoulder and began to explain about how they'd come across it and how the photographer worked for the police department as a patrol officer.

"So cool. I love photography."

Tiegen approached with some beers.

"How did you get involved with forensic photography?" Mitch asked as he guided her to the long couch and took the seat next to her.

She looked at each of them as they joined them. Tiegen sat across from her, and Murdock sat on the ottoman right by her legs. They surrounded her, and Mitch could tell it affected Mia when they were so close. Her body language changed, her cheeks became flush, and she averted her gaze from theirs. Hell, he was affected, too.

"I was in college and debating about going into the police academy while I studied forensic technology and lab work. I was doing a combination criminal justice and forensics degree with this special program they offered at the community college. I also love photography and was asked to do some work. One of my professors got me started with a paid internship with the coroner's office working in the lab. But one day their main photographer came down with the stomach flu, and well, they asked me to step in. I did it no problem. My professor is good friends with Jethro, and both men kind of guided me toward this combination career."

"So did you attend the academy?" Mitch asked "Because I noticed you carry a gun and other technicians don't."

"I went through a special training and have qualifications that allow me to carry and to have the authority of an investigator. From time to time, I'm asked to profile cases and come up with connections. I like being able to carry. But how about you guys? What made you choose to become detectives and enlist in the military?"

"I was in the Marines for five years and then wanted out. I took a series of tests for local, state, and even federal positions that I qualified for and then was brought in under a new division with the state police," Tiegen said to her.

She uncrossed her legs and then re-crossed them. Mitch reached over and ran his hand along her knee and thigh.

"I always wanted to be in law enforcement. Did a youth program through the police department when I was in high school then took the test for the academy and got hired at twenty-one. I worked my way up and constantly take training classes and attend seminars to better my abilities. Homicide investigation is a calling, but it takes a unique person to hunt killers."

He kissed her neck, and Mia closed her eyes and leaned back.

Murdock moved off the ottoman and placed his hands on either side of her thighs.

"I'm into a different kind of hunting. Life-and-death situations. Unlike my brothers' jobs, mine entails figuring out who the enemy is, what they look like, and learning when they're going to strike then stopping them before they get a chance."

Mitch opened his eyes as he heard Mia moan softly and then glanced down to see Murdock uncrossing her legs and pressing her skirt up. He caressed her thighs up and down.

"Sounds dangerous, Murdock. Are you ever scared that you won't find them in time and they'll succeed in hurting people?" she asked him.

He gripped her thighs and lowered his face between her legs to kiss her inner thigh and arouse her pussy.

"I'm very good at hunting. I can sniff out exactly what I'm looking for and what I want."

Mia gasped as Murdock used his teeth to pull on her panties. He looked up as she looked down, and Mitch felt his cock harden beneath his jeans.

"I know what I want right now, and that's to taste you."

Her lips parted, and she gripped the couch on either side of her.

"Let me bring you pleasure, baby, and taste how sweet you are?"

Mitch suckled against her neck, and she moaned. Then he felt her jerk and gasp, and he knew that Murdock was doing as he'd said he would.

He felt her shift upward and then sensed Murdock removing her panties.

"Damn, baby, you taste so good."

"Oh God. Oh, Murdock," she whispered and began to thrust slowly upward.

Mitch pulled his lips from her neck and reached over to undo her blouse and cup her breast. She looked at him, her dark-blue eyes glistening with arousal as he leaned over and kissed her lips. He pulled on her nipple and then plunged his tongue deeper as Murdock feasted on her cunt.

* * * *

Tiegen watch in awe and hoped that Mia would begin to let down the walls and trust them to take care of her. Whatever had occurred in her life to make her feel as if she couldn't succeed in a relationship would be dealt with later. Right now, he wanted to taste her, too.

He moved off the chair and joined his brothers on the couch.

Murdock lifted her thighs up over his shoulders as he fingered Mia's cunt and then alternated tongue and finger. She was moaning and panting, holding on to Mitch as he suckled her breast.

"Damn, you're so wet, Mia. You taste delicious," Murdock told her, and she cried out a release. He continued to feast on her until Tiegen had enough of watching and wanted to join in.

* * * *

Mia couldn't believe how wild she felt. She was thrusting her hips, clawing at Mitch's back as he feasted on her breast while Murdock fingered and sucked her cunt. She couldn't hold back, and she didn't want to. She wanted to feel more.

"I need to taste her, too." Tiegen knelt on the couch and reached for her chin. He held her gaze with eyes as intense looking as she felt.

He covered her mouth, kissing her deeply, and then when he released her lips, he lifted her chin.

"You'll let me taste you, too, and then Mitch?"

She nodded so quickly she felt the heat of embarrassment hit her cheeks. Where had the fear, the anxiety about the inevitable and failing relationships gone to? It was nonexistent when these three men touched her, kissed her, and aroused her body, making her needy for cock and the deep connection only sex could bring.

Slowly her legs lowered, and Murdock gave her a wink as he moved back and Tiegen took his place. She gasped as Tiegen massaged her calves as he knelt between them, and then he gripped her ankles as he held her gaze. He gave them a squeeze. He looked so sexy, intense, and capable that it made her pussy spasm more cream.

"I want you naked on our bed tonight. I want you to put the past behind you, along with everything that ever made you feel like you couldn't love or be loved, and forget it. For tonight, for this moment, Mia, just let go and we'll catch you."

His words brought tears to her eyes but also seemed to bring an encouragement or a push, a challenge, that fed her needs.

She held his gaze and took unsteady breaths as she absorbed the feel of his hard, warm palms moving from her ankles to her inner thighs, spreading her wider.

"Oh God, Tiegen. You make it seem so simple."

Mitch clutched her chin and tilted it toward him. "It is that simple. Nothing but us together, tonight, matters. Let go and let us make you feel so good."

Mitch didn't give her a chance to respond. Instead, he kissed her deeply, plunged his tongue inside, and tasted her fully as thick, hard fingers undid her blouse and her bra the rest of the way. Then she felt the thick, hard digit press up into her cunt. A thumb, Tiegen's, stroked her pussy lips while he thrust fingers to her cunt. He rolled her cream over her pussy lips, round and round, applying the precise amount of pressure to make her inner muscles tighten, her core ache, and tiny spasms erupt and leak more cream. She was sopping wet and felt so needy for cock she wanted it now.

"I need you. Please. More," she begged.

"We want you, too, baby. Feel how badly," Mitch told her as he moved her hand over his cock. Then Murdock did the same with her other hand and brought it to his cock. She cupped their balls, leaned her head back, and moaned out another release as Tiegen suckled and fingered her pussy.

It was too much. She shook and cried out.

"My turn," Mitch said, and Tiegen slowly pulled fingers and tongue from her pussy and moved back.

Mitch immediately took his place and went right in for a taste. He suckled so hard with his lips and tongue that she gasped and grabbed onto his hair and head. She rocked her hips against his mouth and cried out for more.

"Condoms?" Tiegen said aloud.

"Fuck. Upstairs," Murdock said.

"I'm on birth control. I'm safe." She panted for breath.

Mitch pulled back and began to undo his pants. She ran her fingers and hands along his shoulders and grabbed for his shirt, lifting it up over his head as he clumsily got out of his jeans and boxers.

"Upstairs on the bed. We should go now," Tiegen said.

Mitch stopped, and she shook her head.

"Here. Now. Like this." They helped her get her clothes off as she started to do it herself and kept falling back. She was so aroused and needy she just wanted them inside of her now.

"Are you sure?" Mitch asked, stroking his cock in his hand.

Her legs were spread wide, her ass and pussy hung off the couch, and she knew this was right. "Yes, now, Mitch. I need you."

"Fuck." He gripped her hips and aligned his cock with her pussy as he held her gaze.

"So beautiful. This is going to be fast, baby. You got me there already you're so sexy. I promise to make it last longer the next time." He said his last syllables through clenched teeth as he pushed his cock between her pussy lips, nudging to get farther into her tight cunt.

She gripped his shoulders. It had been so long, too long to not feel this connection, this feeling of being overwhelmed. But she realized immediately that she never felt like this. Never desired with this much hunger and an almost carnal instinct to fuck and be fucked. That was what they were doing right now. That was what she needed and wanted.

"Oh." She moaned as he sank his thick, hard cock all the way to what felt like her womb. He grabbed her hips, clenched his teeth, and began to move. He rocked his hips into her. Her breasts bobbed and swayed, only for Tiegen and Murdock to cup them and then feast on them as Mitch stroked his cock faster and faster into her pussy.

They were moaning, and she was trying to catch her breath when Tiegen covered her lips and kissed her deeply. At the same time her pussy spasmed cream, and then she felt fingers stroking her anus and push right in.

She pulled from Tiegen's mouth and cried out her orgasm.

"Fuck, her ass is so tight. It's as tight as her pussy."

"Her ass?" Tiegen asked.

Mitch thrust again and again into her cunt. "Getting it ready for cock. We're making her all ours tonight. All ours forever."

He thrust again and again as he stroked both a finger in her ass and cock in her pussy until he found his release and came.

Mitch moved forward and kissed her lips. He held her cheeks and devoured her moans as she slowly came down from the first round of sex.

As he pulled back and stood up, Tiegen pulled her into his arms and kissed her deeply. She wrapped her arms around him and then lowered over his cock as he lay back on the couch. He gripped her hips.

"I love the tattoo. I love this round ass and sexy body." He used his hands to enforce his words while exploring her body.

He trailed them up her ribs to her breasts then to her cheeks and neck as she rocked up and down on his shaft while gripping his shoulders.

"You're beautiful. You're exceptional." He teased her lips, poked his tongue between them, and pulled back, making her nearly beg for more of his taste. She never felt so desirable and also so ready and willing to please. She rocked faster until she felt Murdock move behind her and begin to rub her back, her spine, and then he caressed her ass cheeks wider.

"Oh." She moaned.

"I think your ass is going to be one of my favorite parts of you," Murdock said, and she felt his lips kissing along her ass.

She lifted up a little higher, and Tiegen lifted her from his waist spread his thighs, opening her, and then she felt the tongue against her anus.

"Murdock," she exclaimed, and her body erupted. She fell forward against his chest. Tiegen suckled her breast as Murdock explored her ass with his fingers. He stroked a digit up into her, and she shivered, shocked at the sensations she felt.

"Oh God. Oh, it burns. It feels so strange." She squealed as Tiegen nipped her nipple and tugged. Her pussy leaked some more. She absorbed every sensation and lost control of her breathing with the feel of Murdock's one hand on her hips and ass and then another hand over the crack of her ass as he thrust fingers in and out of her ass.

She cried out again.

She imagined what she looked like, thrusting on top of Tiegen as Murdock stroked her ass. She felt so sexy and beautiful, like some goddess lover. It was empowering, and she rode it out as her orgasm hit her again.

"I want more," Tiegen said.

"I do, too," Murdock added, and Tiegen pulled her down to kiss her lips as he thrust his cock up into her pussy. She felt so out of control and so full as both men thrust and stroked her. Tiegen's cock felt thicker, harder than before, and Murdock's fingers slid in and out of her ass.

She looked to the right and saw Mitch returning from wherever he'd gone. He held something in his hand.

"Here," he said to Murdock.

Tiegen gripped her cheeks, and she held his gaze and then gasped as Murdock pulled his fingers from her anus.

"We want to take you together. Are you up for it?" Tiegen asked her.

Was she up for it? She'd never felt so aroused, so hot and needy ever. She nodded.

"Say it," he scolded as he pulled her lips closer to his.

His dark eyes were mesmerizing, and the seriousness, the commanding tone, did a number to her body. The way Tiegen held her under her arms, his thumbs hard against the underside of her breasts as he gave her a light shake was so arousing she felt more cream drip. "Yes. I want this. All three of you inside me together."

She tightened up as she felt the cool liquid against her anus.

A hand gripped her shoulder, and then lips kissed her cheek, all while fingers stroked into her ass.

"This will make it easier. A little lube so your tight virgin ass is slick and ready for my cock."

"Oh God." She moaned and felt her body erupt again. With each easy stroke of lubed fingers into her ass, she felt the tiny vibrations of desire grow stronger and stronger. She actually felt her pussy lips swell and a pull deep within her grow so strong, so foreign, that she tightened up.

"Relax those muscles. Let us in," Murdock commanded. "You're going to be all ours."

She'd never had so many mini orgasms and even regular orgasms during sex. She always held back. She never let go. But for some reason, getting triple teamed like this left no room for fears, for inadequacies, or for failure. These men challenged her, broke down her defenses and her fears, and forced her to let go and feel the power of this attraction between them all. She suddenly wanted more, to feel more and to feel whole. She just needed to take this chance.

"More." She moaned, and Tiegen thrust upward as Murdock pulled her hips back and stroked his fingers deeper.

Then she felt Tiegen's lips kissing hers. He explored her mouth and cupped her breasts while Mitch began to kiss her shoulder, her neck, and ear, giving her tiny sexual goose bumps under her skin and all over her body. She shook, and she tightened then loosened and came again.

"Now," Tiegen said, and Mitch gripped her hair and cheeks. He caressed her face, moved her hair from her eyes, and leaned down to kiss her. Once, twice, little pecks of adoration, desire came, expressed in his lips. "I need you, too."

She wasn't quite registering what he meant. How could she? What could she do? She could hardly move she was so aroused.

He brought her head lower, and she understood. With his other hand, he held his cock, and she licked her lips.

"Sweet Jesus, baby, I need you now. Together," he said, and she lowered her mouth to take a taste.

Just as she began to suck him down, to absorb every scent of his manliness, every sensation of being dominated like this, as well as doing some dominating herself, she felt Murdock's fingers pull from her ass. She was shocked at the feeling of loss, but then came the tip of his cock. She sensed it, felt the large, thick bulbous head as it stretched her anus open wider before sinking into her ass with a plop.

She focused on Tiegen's thrusts and Mitch's strokes into her mouth, the way Mitch caressed her hair and played with her breast. She felt sensual, and then came the deep immense feelings of being whole, and she felt the tears roll down her cheeks.

Mitch came first, Tiegen followed, and then she gasped and moaned as she came with Murdock.

It was empowering, overwhelming, like some out-of-body experience because the emotions and power were so foreign to her she was shocked, and she cried. She cried and hugged Tiegen.

"Mia? Are you okay?" Murdock asked as he slid from her ass and laid kisses against her back.

"Mia. Talk to us. Did we hurt you?" Mitch asked then caressed her hair from her cheeks.

She inhaled against Tiegen's neck, absorbed the smell of his cologne and the acceptance of being taken by these three men, brothers, men who represented so much and affected her like no one in her life ever.

"Easy, baby. Easy breaths. You were amazing. What we have is amazing, honey. I knew it," Tiegen said.

She hugged him tighter and kissed his neck, nuzzled against him, so desperate for more of what they made her feel. It was overwhelming. She sensed everything, including the feel of their bare skin pressed together, his muscles pressed to her breasts, her belly, and their hands caressing her back, her ass, and thighs.

"I told you we would catch you, didn't I, baby?" he asked as he pulled her gently back to look her in the eyes.

She couldn't hide the tears, the raw emotions they tore from her wall of steel.

He gave a soft smile. "You're the most beautiful woman I've ever seen. Ever."

She chuckled and wiped her eyes. "I'm a teary-eyed mess, Tiegen." She sniffled.

"You look pretty damn perfect to me," Mitch added, and she looked at him and rubbed more tears from her eyes and cheeks.

She felt Murdock's hands on her shoulders. She tilted her head back to lock gazes with him. He caressed his hand along her throat in a sexy, possessive manner then gripped her chin.

"It was magical. I felt it, too. This is special, baby. Don't think for once it isn't."

He leaned down and pressed his lips to hers, and she hoped what he said was true. Because now that she had a taste of what it felt like to feel whole, protected, part of something and someone, she wanted to continue to feel it and never let that go.

Chapter 5

Murdock explored Mia's body with his lips and fingers. She lay on the bed between Mitch and Tiegen after making love once again.

He licked along the path of her tattoo, complimenting her artwork before suckling her hip bone. She giggled and swatted at his arm.

"That tickles," she reprimanded, but then she yawned. He climbed up her body, and Tiegen moved to the side, making some room.

"Murdock."

She moaned as he pressed his body over hers, his cock nice and hard and ready to make love again, despite being at it all night. It was late, two a.m., but he didn't want to waste time sleeping when he could mark Mia as his woman in every way.

He pressed between her legs, and she ran her fingers through his hair. He turned his face to kiss her belly.

"I love your body. How fit and voluptuous you are," he whispered, and his warm breath caused little goose bumps to emerge over her skin.

"I love your body, too. You have a lot of little scars." She traced some on his shoulders.

He kissed over her belly button. "It comes with the territory," he said then lowered down and licked her pussy. She tasted like soap and his bodywash. Mitch had been sure to lather her up nice and good when they took a break from making love to hit the showers and get refreshed.

She gripped his shoulders tighter. "Is what you do dangerous?"

He nipped her groin. "Yes," he teased, and she shivered.

"You're a Marine?"

He stroked her clit and tugged on it then held her gaze as he trailed his tongue up her belly to her nipple. "Special Forces." He tugged on the little pink bud as he raised her arms above her head.

"Oh God."

Mitch and Tiegen chuckled.

"He's seen a lot of crazy shit. Never tells us anything." Tiegen leaned closer, sitting up and caressing her hair along the pillow.

Murdock thought she looked like a goddess. Her large breasts pushed forward while her hips and ass were forced down by the weight of his body. He sat up, clasped his fingers with hers, and kept them raised above her head. Everything about her turned Murdock on and made him feel protective and possessive of her.

He rocked his hips slowly as they stared into one another's eyes.

"Do you still go on dangerous secret missions?" she asked.

Mitch leaned on his elbow on the other side of her and ran his finger over her nipple.

She gasped and lifted her hips upward.

"Yes. But probably not for a while."

"What? Why not?" Tiegen asked him, and Murdock saw his brothers' reactions to his statement.

He usually went from one mission to the next, always taking on whatever was available, no matter how dangerous. But after the last few missions, and the close calls he had, Murdock realized that he couldn't count on other people to do their job to the fullest like he always did. Worrying about your partner, your troop, and losing focus, even for a split second, could mean the difference between living and dying. He'd had it with that fear.

He looked at Tiegen. "I'm thinking about retiring completely."

"Seriously?" Mitch asked, and Murdock smiled.

Murdock knew his brothers worried about him.

"Yes. I've had it with a lot of things, and mostly the violence." He released Mia's hands and then massaged down her chest, cupping and squeezing her breasts then massaging over her ribs to her hips. He held her gaze.

"I'm thinking there are more important things to focus on. New incentives to end being in the center of danger."

Tiegen caressed Mia's cheek and turned her face toward him. He smiled.

"I know what you mean. Mia is quite special." He kissed her softly, and then Murdock saw her expression change. He felt her tighten up.

"Mia?"

"I don't know what to say. I feel incredible when I'm with the three of you. Tonight has been amazing."

"Why does there sound like a but is in there somewhere?" Mitch asked, sitting up.

She hugged herself and rubbed her arms. Murdock could see the struggle in her eyes, sense that she was really fearful still about this relationship. He wanted to know why. What could it be that made her hold back?

"Talk to us, Mia. Don't hold it in. Tell us why you're so resistant to a commitment with us. I know it's our first night together, but damn, baby, I don't care how possessive or chauvinistic I sound. I don't want you to leave. I don't want to even consider another day without you in our lives. This house never felt so complete," Tiegen told her, and her eyes filled up with tears.

"That's so beautiful, Tiegen. You make me feel like anything is possible."

"Anything is possible in a relationship like this, with feelings this strong so instant," Mitch added.

Murdock caressed her arms. "Why don't you tell us why you're so resistant? It could help us understand."

She looked at them, and then she lowered her eyes.

"I guess there are a lot of reasons. Losing my parents when I was young and having to work to put myself through college and rent an apartment was hard. I learned pretty quickly to rely on myself."

"That's so tough, Mia. I couldn't imagine having to go through that. What I can tell you is that we're your family now. We'll take care of you, protect you, and we have a lot of relatives and family, too," Tiegen said to her. She smiled.

"Did you have friends around at all?" Mitch asked her.

"In college." She started moving, and he lifted so she could sit up. She reached for the pillow and placed it in front of her to cover her body. Murdock felt his chest tighten with concern.

"What happened in college?" Tiegen asked.

She turned toward him. "What do you mean?"

Tiegen caressed her arm. "You tensed up. Covered yourself from us."

"Your body language changed," Mitch told her.

"Explain it so we understand," Murdock said to her. He caressed her thigh as she sat with her legs tucked under her.

She swallowed hard.

* * * *

Mia wasn't sure how to explain things to them. She worried about them thinking she was emotionally unstable. But really that wasn't the case. She had accepted, to a point, what happened to Wynona. It had been motivation to get into the forensics field and to hunt people like the one who'd killed Wynona.

She took a deep breath and looked at them. Mitch, Tiegen, and Murdock were exceptional men. Just looking at them made her body hum with such adoration and desire. It was a lot to digest.

"Mia, just talk to us, baby. What happened to make you feel like you have to keep this wall up?" Tiegen asked her as he caressed her thigh.

"You asked me why I got involved in forensics and photography. You talked to me about your callings and how each of you was drawn to your profession. Well, for me, it was a combination of witnessing my parents suffer with illness that eventually killed them and knowing that I was adopted. Somewhere out there were my biological parents. I started thinking about trying to find them. You know, DNA testing, tracking them down. But as I learned more about the science of DNA, about forensic evidence and leaving behind literally parts of you wherever you go, whether that be a hair follicle or fingerprint or even blood, it drew me in. I began to really get an understanding of forensics and investigating crimes. I was accepted into the police academy but wasn't sure that was the route I wanted to take. My professor guided me through the process in my final year of college when the second thing happened to make me go this professional route."

She took a breath and felt the anxiety in telling them once again.

"And what was that?" Murdock asked, kneeling in front of her and holding her gaze.

"Coming home to my apartment and learning that my roommate and best friend had been abducted."

"What?" Tiegen asked.

She nodded and began to ramble on about what happened.

"It was a crime scene in no time. The apartment was turned upside down, and eventually, the detectives thought that it was indeed an abduction by someone she knew. They questioned so many people and guys she had been seen with. But eventually, days later, it led to someone finding a high-heeled shoe in the woods and Wynona's bloody blouse."

"Damn. Did they find out what happened, and who did it?" Mitch asked her.

She looked at him. "No. They organized search parties, and we all searched the woods near where the blouse and shoe were found. It was thirty minutes away from our apartment, deep in the woods. It was so crazy. But I'll never forget the moment I saw her. I practically stumbled over her the brush was so thick." She looked toward the wall and away from them.

She felt the hand on her shoulder then Tiegen caressing her hair.

"You found your roommate's body?"

She nodded.

"Jesus." Murdock cupped her cheeks and held her.

"That breaks my heart, baby. No one should have to view something like that. God, you've been through hell."

She felt the stray tear leak from her eye.

"It's why I'm able to do what I do though. I can make the separation. I don't get emotionally involved because of my experiences. A therapist at the academy said that, because of my lack of feeling loved and, instead, feeling abandoned by my parents, my adoptive parents, and then forcibly abandoned by Wynona, that this wall inside is to help protect myself instead of projecting what I do back onto me. I guess I've never had a person to rely on, and in order to not feel pain, sadness like I did at finding Wynona's body, and the fact that I've had to handle everything myself and could never rely on anyone to stick around. I created a defense mechanism."

"It's not fair. No one should have to feel so alone." Murdock pressed his lips to hers and gently kissed her.

"You're not alone anymore. We're here for you," Tiegen said as Murdock released her.

"I don't know if I can give you more than what I did tonight."

"It's okay, baby. We'll take things slow. You'll start to realize that we're the real deal and that we're not going anywhere." Mitch said to her next.

"What about R.J.? How does he fit into all of this?" Tiegen asked her.

She could tell he was already jealous of the guy, but she needed to tell them the truth.

"R.J. was one of the detectives working the case. He was older, was there when my apartment was turned into a crime scene investigation and nearby when I found Wynona's body."

"So he hit on you?" Tiegen asked with an angry tone as he stood up and paced a little.

"No, Tiegen. Things between us just happened. I was scared, I was going through so much emotional crap, and then R.J. became my rock. He taught me how to defend myself and how to get over Wynona's murder. Then we spent more and more time together, and eventually things happened."

"Why did you break up?" Mitch asked her. She glanced at him and then took a little breath.

"I couldn't give him what he wanted." She looked down at the pillow to avoid their eyes.

She felt the fingers under her chin and tilted up to see Murdock. He appeared so masculine and intense. He was a soldier who had seen so much in his career, including dead bodies like she had.

"What did he want that you couldn't give him?" Murdock asked.

She felt the tears in her eyes and also the pain of the words she was about to say. Because in this moment, with the three of them around her and feeling the connection to them after having sex so many times, she realized they already meant so much more to her. She could see herself falling in love with them, and that was stupid, crazy, and would only lead to her getting hurt.

"My heart. I couldn't let down the walls entirely and let him in. Eventually we grew apart and ended it as I graduated from college and took a job with Jethro."

"But he called you the other day. You still talk to him?" Tiegen asked.

"I hadn't spoken with him in a couple of years."

"So why now? He wants to rekindle a romance?" Mitch asked.

"I don't know. He was working on a case, and when he started saying he wanted to meet to talk, I got a call to respond to a homicide. So I don't know yet."

"You're not getting together with him," Tiegen told her.

She tilted her head at him, giving him a sympathetic expression.

"Do you really think that something would happen between R.J. and me now after what we just shared? I haven't slept with another man in years, and I let down my guard. I accepted your promise of taking things slow and catching me as I let go, and now you don't trust me?"

He held her gaze. "We're taking a risk, too. We don't go around sharing women all the time. In fact, with Murdock gone so much, we started drifting apart a bit until you came along." He stomped closer, pressed one knee to the bed, and cupped her cheeks between his hands, making the pillow fall from her body. His expression was hard, serious, determined as he stared down into her eyes and at her lips then breasts. He held her gaze. "I want you in every way. We all do. You've got me so riled up, feeling so needy to claim every inch of you and mark you as our woman in every possible way so no other men can have what belongs to us, and that's you. I've never felt like this. So possessive, protective, and, hell, caveman-like."

"You're not kidding," Mitch added, and Murdock mumbled.

She placed her hands over Tiegen's and gave him a sincere, honest expression.

"Don't be jealous. I'm scared, too. I'm scared that I'll screw this all up because of my past."

"Honey, you've made the first step by letting us in and letting us fuck you in lust, desire, and these out-of-control and powerful emotions that are running through the four of us. But now, now is different. Now, we're making love to you because this relationship, this connection, is so much fucking more." His explicit words shocked her, and then fact that he said they would now make love to her instantly warmed her heart, and she actually felt the walls of fear and mistrust begin to break down. Tiegen covered her mouth and kissed her. She felt the pillow being pushed aside, and then Tiegen lay her down and made love to her mouth. Tender kiss after tender kiss, she sank down deeper into the mattress and allowed her feelings to show as she reciprocated Tiegen's caresses.

As he took his time tasting her, teasing her, she ran her fingers through his hair over his shoulders and to his sides as he pressed between her thighs.

He kissed her chin and neck as he pressed her arms and hands above her head and clasped their fingers together. 'I'll never get enough of making love to you, of claiming you in every way."

She felt his cock tap against her pussy. Instantly, the cream leaked, and she pressed upward, trying to get him inside of her. She wanted that connection. She yearned for it and felt how much different this was from earlier. Earlier was carnal, wild, with lustful rounds of sex and satisfying an itch in each of them. This was different, deeper, stronger, and honest.

He lowered down to suckle her breast. She watched his mouth as he feasted on her then tugged her nipple between his teeth. He looked so sexy, so manly as the small veins by his temples pulsed and tightened. The cords of his muscles in his arms flexed as he lifted up, tugging her nipple in the same upward motion, and she moaned. His large hands slid down from her fingers to her elbows and were now at her underarms, holding her in place. It was sexy to be in such a submissive position with a man, with men she trusted. That thought that she indeed trusted them had her closing her eyes and tilting her pussy upward in need.

"Mine always, baby. Always."

He nudged the thick, bulbous head between her pussy lips and slowly sank into her. He prodded and thrust gently, pulling back slightly and then pressing in slightly in a torturous, slow technique that made her thighs quiver and her whole body tighten with arousal. When he finally slid all the way in, they both sighed.

"Sweet heaven. You're perfection, Mia. Perfection." He began to thrust into her over and over again.

She held his gaze and countered his trusts. The motion and speed were slow enough to make her beg for more yet deep enough and good enough to make her want to absorb every stroke and hold on to the sensations forever.

"You look so beautiful, baby," Mitch whispered, taking position on her side. Her lips parted, and she moaned softly as Murdock moved to her other side.

"All ours to love, enjoy, and possess in every way," Murdock told her as Tiegen lifted up, releasing her arms and then pulling her thighs higher and up against his sides.

As he began to increase his pace, Murdock and Mitch lifted her arms and held them above her head. They were all staring down at her body, at her breasts that tingled and her lips that yearned for more of their taste from their lips and their skin, and to her pussy that pulsated and dripped cream, easing Tiegen's strokes and making him move faster.

"I can feast on you for hours, Mia," Murdock told her.

"Me too," Mitch said, and using their mouths, they descended onto her breasts and began to feast on her as Tiegen thrust harder and faster.

She felt so out of control with her arms held down and her body being taken by them, loved by them. She felt those walls begin to break down further and further as they loved her body in every way.

She cried out her first release, and then Murdock and Mitch pulled up as Tiegen thrust faster and faster and came when he called out her name. Murdock and Mitch released her arms, and she hugged Tiegen to her chest.

She was panting with need, still feeling so aroused and wanting Murdock and Mitch to make love to her next as Tiegen pressed his lips to hers and kissed her deeply. He held her gaze.

"Murdock's and then Mitch's turn to make love to you," he said in a tone that was so sexy she shivered.

He eased his cock from her pussy and climbed down off the bed. Murdock took his place and began to caress his hands up her thighs to her hips, squeezing them and kneading them, then moving his hands to her breasts. He leaned forward and kissed her tenderly. He made love to her mouth and nudged his hard cock against her pussy lips, teasing her and making her thrust downward.

"Tell me you want me to make love to you," he said, his lips close to hers, his dark-blue eyes filled with desire and hunger.

"Make love to me, Murdock. I need you, I want you." She felt the gush of emotions flood her heart as he pressed his lips to hers, and she hugged him tight. She felt him lift upward and press his cock between her pussy lips then thrust right in. "Oh, Murdock." She moaned, lips parted, hands clinging to his bare shoulders, the feel of steely muscles and masculinity arousing her pussy even more.

He rocked his hips as he licked her skin and suckled her neck, causing tiny goose bumps to travel below her skin and make her shiver and come again and again. He was relentless in his ministrations, going from suckling her skin as he stroked his cock into her cunt to kissing the corner of her mouth then covering her mouth and plunging his tongue in deeply. It was arousing, and she felt compelled to take more from him, to accept anything and everything he was willing to give. She clung to him harder, lifted her pelvis, and wrapped her thighs higher up around his hips as he lifted and thrust deeper, faster. The bed rocked, and the atmosphere was amazing, indescribable as they both sought out their relief.

"I'm there, baby. Come with me. You're mine always." He suckled her neck as he thrust so fast she could hardly breathe, and she came again. Murdock followed, thrusting, stroking, squeezing her ass cheeks as he rocked his cock harder, deeper until he came.

He lifted up and held her gaze. "You're everything. We'll never abandon you, Mia. Trust me. I've never left a man behind, and I'm certainly never going to leave my woman behind either." His words touched her heart as she hugged him and held him tightly until Murdock lifted up to let Mitch make love to her next.

Tiegen was there with a washcloth to clean her up and dry her gently as Mitch eased by her side and cupped her cheek. She held his gaze and smiled.

"You feel the difference, the power of it all?" he asked.

She nodded. "Yes." He smiled, an authentic, sincere smile that lit up his dark-blue eyes and proved instantly that this was real, he was real.

She rolled over to lie side by side with Mitch. He ran his large, warm palm along her thigh and hip to her waist, pulling her against him. When he kissed her forehead and used this palm to cup her breast then tease her nipple with his thumb, she felt wet and ready to make love to him.

She leaned up to kiss his lips, and he rolled to his back, allowing her to explore his skin the way he and his brothers had explored hers. She rolled her tongue and lips along his neck and the cord of veins lifted from his skin, and he gripped her hips, squeezing her.

The feel of sharp whiskers enticed her arousal as she rubbed back and forth then lifted higher to feel his whiskers against her breasts. Mitch pulled a nipple into his mouth, and she moaned as she reached between them and cupped his sac.

She was rocking her hips, felt her cream drip, and she knew she needed him inside of her.

"So good, baby," he whispered after releasing her breast with a plop.

She felt his fingers press against her pussy, and she moaned, tilting her breasts upward.

"So hot and wet for me, aren't you, Mia?" he asked.

"Yes." She moved her hand from his sac to his cock, stroking it up and down. His fingers felt so good as they drew more cream from her sensitive cunt, making her release another small orgasm.

She rolled him to his back completely and straddled his waist. He pulled his fingers from her cunt, and she aligned his cock with her pussy and eased down onto his shaft.

Mitch held her gaze. She held his shoulders, and they stared at one another as she rode him slowly. Her ass slid over his hips, and he spread his thighs wider as she rocked back and forth, up and down, trying to ease the ache in her cunt but also feed more of the desire to claim him as hers. Her heart soared, and her body convulsed as she came hard, crying out his name.

Mitch immediately rolled her to her back, lifted her thighs higher, and thrust into her hard, fast before taking her arms and holding them above her head. They were spread out over the mattress, and she didn't need to look to know that Murdock and Tiegen were there watching, being just as much a part of this love session. She didn't need them to take her together to know that they were now one. Whether making love separately like this, or together, all inside of her, she knew they were hers and she was theirs. Their bond was so deep, so strong, she felt like nothing could destroy it, not even her fears of being unable to commit fully or give her heart to them fully. For as Mitch came inside of her, calling her name, filling her with his seed, she knew, in that instant, they already had her heart and a part of her soul forever.

Chapter 6

"R.J. We just got a call from his partner. This young woman went missing last night from a bar outside of Portland Place. She matches the description of the others. Brunette, great body, young around twenty-five, classy, working for a law firm."

"Okay, any leads yet as to who may have taken her or evidence of anything like a struggle, et cetera?" R.J. asked him as he stood by his desk thumbing through the files from the other cases.

"There was something left by her car."

"What?"

"A note that said, 'Catch me if you can.'" Mosley told him.

R.J. stopped looking over the files. "What the hell?"

"I know. I think he's starting to taunt us. He knows that we're onto him and we must be getting closer. I've been thinking about the other cases and some of the things left behind and how this guy takes his victims into the woods. Leaves a bloody shoe, and a piece of clothing. They all look so similar, and, well, I ran it against some other cases from years ago, and I came up with a name of a woman who went missing for a year. Her name was Colleen Fayen. She was twenty-two, a college student in Manhattan. In the file, the investigators had notes about her telling her friends about a guy who lived in a nearby apartment building who was sort of bothering her. Anyway as they interviewed the friends, they found out the guy was always watching out for her or acting like he was her security coming in and out of the apartment building. When they tried to find this guy to question him, they couldn't. But sources said the neighbors believed he did odd jobs around the building."

"You mean like a custodian?" R.J. asked.

"Yes, but not all the time, and they didn't think the landlord paid him either. Detectives spoke with the landlord, and he said the guy didn't even live in the apartment building but he lived outside of the city. He liked to hunt, had a cabin or something somewhere between Wellington and Yarland, maybe on the border of Pennsylvania. He wasn't sure, so we would need to check all those places out."

"No clue as to who this guy was, a name or anything?"

"He went by Pete, but that's about it. I'm trying to get in contact with the detectives on that case to see if there was ever a photograph or sketch done of the guy."

"Good. You keep on top of that. I'll look into that case on this end and meet up with you later."

"Sounds good. Did you speak with Mia yet?"

"Not yet, but I'm going to see if any of the other cases indicated a man who worked in the women's apartment buildings was found or questioned. I don't recall that being the case with Wynona's case. She had been taken from the apartment and no one saw a thing, plus the cameras at the time were all broken. It was a crappy apartment building."

"So was this one from how the detectives describe it."

"Probably not a coincidence. Let's touch base later."

R.J. got off the phone and immediately began to search up information on this victim from years ago called Colleen. He immediately found out her last name, Fayen, and all the information that Mosley had explained to him. He tracked down the precinct that had been overseeing the case back then and saw that it was listed as unsolved but remained open. He got the number for the detectives who were now working in the South Bronx in a similar unit doing homicide investigation.

An hour later, he was taking notes and trying to come up with another common factor besides the description of all the women being similar in build, hair color, eye color, and type. In all the cases, there had been talk about a man who worked in their apartments or who was seen on a regular basis or often enough that witnesses mentioned him at the times of the investigations. Could this man be the killer? Who was he? How did he keep evading detection, and was he the one responsible for this latest missing woman? He had to figure it out. And why had the killer left a message this time? Was it because R.J. had been the investigator on all the cases since Wynona's abduction and murder and he was taunting him? Or was this guy getting ready to do something even more extreme? He had too many questions and not enough answers. They had to try and find this latest missing woman. They had to, and hopefully, she would have the answers to who this guy really was.

* * * *

"We don't want you to go yet." Mitch caressed her hair from her cheek and placed the loose strand behind Mia's ear. He held her gaze, feeling his heart ache from the fact that she had to go home to get ready for work tomorrow morning. They had spent the weekend together, making love, enjoying conversation, and getting to know one another. She seemed to be letting her guard down more and more with him and his brothers and he couldn't help but smile as she hugged him around the waist.

"I need to get some sleep and recoup for the week. You guys tired me out." She smiled, a sweet gleam in her eyes.

Murdock placed his hands on her shoulders from behind and pressed up against her.

"You didn't seem too tired thirty minutes ago." He squeezed her hips as he kissed her neck. She closed her eyes, and Mitch kissed her lips. That kiss began to get out of hand quickly as Murdock pressed his hands under her skirt and began to undress her.

She slapped their hands gently and pulled from between them.

She looked so flushed and aroused. "Stop that or I'll never get home."

"Sounds like a plan to me," Tiegen said, arms crossed, staring at her from the doorway.

She gave him a sideways glance, and Mitch chuckled. Tiegen was being the most possessive and not afraid to show it. Mia accepted it with a smile and even tried easing his worry, but Tiegen was a force to be reckoned with.

"I need to go." She pulled her purse strap onto her shoulder. As she turned, Murdock grabbed her hand, pulled her back, then cupped her cheeks and neck and kissed her deeply. She held on to his hands, stood up on tiptoes, and kissed him back.

"Behave," he warned after he released her lips.

"You're the one going hunting," she teased then headed toward the door.

Tiegen stared down at her. "Can we get together tomorrow night after work for dinner?"

"If I don't get caught up in anything."

He looked her over, and she stood there staring up at him. Their brother was big just like him and Murdock. Mia seemed to be able to handle his possessive, aggressive behavior though as she stepped closer and ran her hands along Tiegen's arms and uncrossed them. She placed them around her waist, putting his hands on her ass as she lifted up on tiptoes to kiss him.

His brother stared down into her eyes, not totally allowing her control where his hands went now, a moment before he pressed his lips to hers and kissed her deeply.

Mitch watched his brother's large hands move over Mia's perfect ass and squeeze and massage the cheeks in the sexy skirt she wore. Their woman had a hell of a body on her, and they enjoyed exploring it thoroughly this weekend.

As he released her lips, she sighed.

"Are you sure you can't stay?"

"As badly as I want to, I need the rest and to be on my game. I'll call you guys tomorrow."

She went to move, and he gripped her hips.

"You'll call tonight," he said, and she nodded.

"Yes, sir." She saluted.

He gave her ass a spank.

"Tiegen."

"Watch it, Miss Mallory, or that sexy ass of yours will get a spanking you'll never forget." She blushed as she rubbed her hands down her skirt, and then Mitch opened the door.

"Text me when you get home."

She nodded and headed out the door.

Murdock walked toward the window, watching her leave.

Mitch felt the loss of Mia's presence in their home immediately. He liked her a lot. Hell, he could love her so easily if she would just let down her guard completely. But that would take time.

"What do you think?" Murdock asked his brothers as he took a seat in the living room. They followed.

"I think she's perfect for us," Mitch said to him.

"It was a hell of a weekend," Tiegen stated as he walked over toward the custom bar and took out three glasses then poured some brandy in each of them. Mitch took one of the glasses, and Tiegen brought one over to Murdock, and then he took his and joined his brothers.

"To a hell of a weekend." Mitch raised his glass.

"To many more with Mia," Murdock added, and they clinked the glasses and downed the brandy.

They were all silent, and Mitch spoke first. "Damn, it feels empty without her here."

"It's crazy, isn't it?" Murdock added.

"It sure is. Things have changed literally overnight. But this is new, and Mia has a lot of emotions to work out," Tiegen said.

"I know you're worried. Hell, you're still jealous about this R.J. guy, aren't you?"

"And you aren't, Mitch?" Tiegen asked.

"Listen, we've had lovers. We're a lot older than Mia and more experienced, and we don't want her feeling jealous about any of that. We should focus on the four of us and the relationship we've started. Nothing else matters," Murdock said to them.

"But she's going to see this guy. He could try to rekindle a romance, hell, get her in bed, kiss her, or make her confused about taking this chance with us. We know how complicated and special a ménage relationship is, and she could get cold feet," Tiegen said.

"But we have to trust her like we asked her to trust us. If we overwhelm her and don't give her space, it could turn her off. She feels the same attraction and desire, and she didn't want to leave. We need to take this time to process it all and figure out what's next," Mitch said.

"Her moving in with us so she's in our bed with one of us deep inside of her every night ensuring she's ours forever," Tiegen said, and Mitch and Murdock chuckled.

"Jeesh, Tiegen, I've never seen you like this," Murdock said to him, smiling.

"I've never felt like this. My gut is clenching right now with worry because she's not here where I can ensure she's safe and never gets hurt or feels pain again. What she went through, the lack of love and being abandoned like that, never mind finding her best friend's dead body, just kills me inside. I want her to feel important and cared for. She deserves it."

"She sure does, and we'll have our chance because of the results we had this weekend. It wasn't a fuck fest, Tiegen. We made love to her. We saw that love reciprocated in her eyes. This is real," Mitch added.

"Real enough that I'm thinking some serious changes are in order," Murdock told them.

"Changes?" Tiegen asked. He stood up, walked over to the bar to grab the bottle of brandy, then brought it over to fill their glasses.

"I've been thinking things through for a while, and whether this works out with Mia or not, I'm going to hand in my papers and retire from Special Forces."

"Seriously?" Mitch asked.

Murdock held his gaze. "The last several missions were bad. People don't have one another's backs anymore, and leaving a man behind is a sacrifice that has become too real of a possibility lately. I can't do that to you guys and certainly not to Mia. You two will be happy to know that I spoke with Chief Riley, as well as Damien and his brothers. I have some options for work lined up, and it makes my decision to leave the Corps easier."

They stared at Murdock, and Mitch couldn't help but feel relieved and happy.

He raised his glass. "To whatever decision you make, we have your back."

"That's for shit sure." Tiegen raised his glass.

Murdock placed his glass against theirs. "To Mia."

"To Mia," they all said, clinking their glasses together and downing the brandy.

Mitch smiled wide. They were finally going to have the family they always wanted and the woman of their dreams that completed them. His brother Murdock was here to stay, and the fears and worries of him returning in a body bag would be distant memories, in the past, and one less fear to live with day after day. All because of Mia.

* * * *

An hour later, as Mia sat by her desk in the office, her cheeks still felt heated. She had been bombarded with questions from Amy and Alyssa the moment she arrived to work that morning. By the looks she got from Reed, it was pretty obvious that everyone knew she hadn't made it into Crossroads Friday night and had been gone for the weekend.

Apparently it was Amy who told Murdock and Mitch that she'd been being mauled by their brother in the parking lot and that they might need to intervene. The girls got a chuckle out of that one, but ultimately, they were happy for her.

She couldn't stop thinking about Mitch, Tiegen, and Murdock or how it felt to make love to them together and separately. There was still a fear of screwing things up and not being sure that things would work out between them, but she felt it was a natural response in any new relationship. After all, it had been years since she'd been involved with R.J., and she'd been young, inexperienced, and in a state of turmoil at the time. But she hadn't regretted it. She just regretted hurting R.J.

She looked at her cell phone and wondered why he hadn't called her back and what he needed from her in regards to a case they were working on. But then, her phone buzzed, and she heard others go off around the office. A homicide. It was time to go to work.

* * * *

R.J. pulled onto the scene along with Mosley. They had traveled the twenty-five minutes to get to the crime scene, knowing that this was probably their latest victim. The serial killer had struck again, and R.J. already had calls into friends of his in the FBI. They were on their way, too, and they knew of the other cases, as well as Wynona's.

As they got out of their car and approached the crime scene, R.J. noticed Mia right away. She wore a snug-fitting pair of black dress pants and a warm sweater that couldn't hide her voluptuous breasts. He felt that mix of emotions, the love he had for her a long time ago and the connection they would always have since he had been her first lover.

"R.J.?" Mosley said to him.

"Is that her?" he added. R.J. nodded, and Mosley whistled low. "Wow."

R.J. felt that little hint of jealousy knowing how attractive Mia was and how instantly her body gained men's attention.

As she finished up, and he and Mosley walked closer, introducing themselves to the detectives on the scene, she caught his eye. But then she looked away from him and at two detectives there. Mosley introduced them to the two men, who looked as though they could be related.

"We're Detectives Mosley Lane and R.J. Duncan," Mosley said as he stuck out his hand to shake theirs.

They hesitated a moment, looked at Mia, and then back at them.

"Investigator Tiegen McKay and Detective Mitch McKay."

"Brothers?" Mosley asked, and then men nodded.

They went over the case so far and about the woman found murdered, her body left by a ravine and tunnel outside a wooded area nearby. They walked over to go over the scene, but R.J. kept glancing at Mia as she took more pictures and then packed up and spoke with the medical examiner from the CI unit she worked with.

As they went over some other information and Mosley filled them in, R.J. took the moment to walk over to Mia as she placed her things into the truck.

"Mia."

She turned to look up at him. She looked stunning, happy, and he felt as if he'd been punched in the gut. He didn't want her to look unhappy or even miserable. He had just wanted her to feel something for him still, despite the nearly two years that had passed since they were lovers.

"R.J."

He stepped closer, pulled her into an embrace, and hugged her tightly. As he looked past her shoulder, he saw the detectives watching, and both looked pissed. He had an uneasy feeling inside as he pulled back but focused on Mia.

"You look beautiful as always," he told her as he released her.

She smiled. "Thanks. It's terrible to meet you again under these circumstances, but I guess considering our professions it was liable to happen." She sounded so sophisticated, older and more confident. He just stared at her, and her cheeks reddened, and she started fixing her things. He chuckled and leaned his hand on his gun and holster.

"How have you been? You look incredible. I've heard such great things about your abilities and photographic talent."

"Really? Well, that's good to know. I've been well, R.J. And you? Is this homicide connected to something you're working on?"

"Actually, we need to talk. Mosley, my partner, and I have been pulling some information together, and there seems to be some links with our other cases."

"And you think this one is, too?" she asked, stepping to the side and crossing her arms in front of her chest. She seemed so professional. He was impressed.

"Well, we'll know after your team gathers some evidence. Is there someplace we can meet up to talk later and go over some things?"

She hesitated and looked past him. He followed her line of sight and saw the one investigator, Tiegen, keeping an eye on things. Perhaps she was seeing him.

"If your boyfriend doesn't mind," he said to her, and she opened her mouth to speak, and then she smirked.

"Okay, Detective Duncan. You have my cell number. Let me know what works for you. I'll also get you copies of the pictures if it helps at all."

"That would be great." But he didn't ask her any questions or indicate that this case and his others may have a connection to Wynona's murder. He still wasn't sure, and he knew the killer had left a message for him on purpose. He stopped her from walking away by placing his hand over her arm. She stopped and swallowed hard. He released her arm.

"Listen, it's important that we meet and talk."

"What's going on R.J.?" she asked as Mosley, Tiegen, and Mitch joined them. Mitch and Tiegen took positions on either side of Mia, and R.J. had an instant funny sensation.

"You guys met right?" she asked.

"Yes we did," R.J said.

"So you were saying something about a connection in the cases," Mia said, and R.J. began to explain what they had thus far and also about the person who worked in the building that no one seemed to be able to identify. They were still working on getting an image of the guy.

"Mia, there may be a connection to Wynona's case."

She tightened up. Immediately, Tiegen placed his arm around her waist.

"What do you mean?" Mitch asked. It was obvious that these two men knew about Wynona so they must be important to Mia. Which one was she seeing? he wondered.

"We're not a hundred percent sure yet, but aside from these women looking so much alike and similar evidence left behind, there's been another common factor. A man witnesses say was working in the buildings the women lived in. It was someone who wasn't on the books but helped out. We can't track him down from any cases. Do you remember anyone from your building, Mia? Anyone that the two of you would see from time to time helping out and that maybe Wynona spoke with?"

Mia looked as though she was thinking about that a moment.

"I don't recall anyone. But then again, it was originally Wynona's place, and I was always at the college either at class or working until late. I barely spoke to any of the neighbors. Do you really think the same man who took her and killed her could be the one involved in these other murders?"

"We're leaning toward that because, as we backtracked in every case, witnesses described a man who worked as a custodian or helper around the apartments. In every case, there was no other information and no pictures of the guy, only some descriptions," Mosley said.

"Damn, if someone could get their hands on a picture, it could help us track the guy down," Mitch said.

"We're working on it," R.J. said.

"Well, I need to get back to the office and run these pictures." She held R.J.'s gaze.

"I'll call you in a little while. We'll talk."

She nodded.

"Anything you need, we'll be here to assist you. If it is the same person that killed Mia's roommate, we want to help out," Tiegen told them.

"Thank you. We'll be in touch once the coroner comes up with his findings and we have Mia's people do their thing," R.J. said to him.

R.J. and Mosley walked back toward the crime scene area and to Jethro to discuss any possible evidence left behind. A quick glance over his shoulder and he saw Tiegen slide his hand from her waist to her ass before he walked away. He also saw Mitch say something to her, and she nodded. But then Mia looked toward him and the crime scene. He hoped she would be okay and that this wouldn't bring back the nightmares she used to have.

"So which one do you think she's with?" Mosley asked him.

"Not sure."

"Could be both," Mosley replied, and R.J. was a bit surprised, but then again, ménage relationships were rampant around these parts.

Perhaps she was with both of them. He was a little disappointed, but he knew he and Mia weren't meant to be together. What they had was special at the time, but maybe the walls she had surrounding her heart took the power of more than one man to break down. It just sort of hurt to know that he hadn't been the one to do so.

* * * *

"You're not meeting him," Mitch told her. She walked over to Mitch's police SUV along with Tiegen the moment Jethro walked away.

She looked around them, and no one seemed to be paying attention to them talking.

"Mitch, it's not a big deal. He just wants to talk and go over the connections with the case and the fact that these murders could be connected to Wynona's death."

"He still has feelings for you," Tiegen whispered firmly.

"I doubt that." She looked over her shoulder and spotted R.J. and Mosley talking to two federal agents who arrived moments ago.

"You didn't see him looking at your ass, drooling," Tiegen countered, raising his voice slightly.

She reached out and caressed his arm. "Please, Tiegen, lower your voice. R.J. isn't like that."

"All men are like that," Mitch added, and she crossed her arms in front of her chest.

"That means you are, too," she countered to Mitch.

"The difference is that your ass belongs to us, not him or any other guy."

She took a deep breath and released it. "You heard what he said, and now with the feds involved, there's a chance we could help find Wynona's killer. I need to meet with him and see what I can do to help."

"I don't like it. We're supposed to hang out later and do dinner when Murdock returns from the woods," Tiegen told her.

She reached out and caressed his hand. "And we'll do that. I promise. If I meet up with R.J., it will only be for a little while."

"Fine, but keep us posted on where you are. In regards to the case, we're going to work with the feds to see if we can get a picture of this guy who worked in the buildings where all these women lived. R.J. said the killer left the message 'catch me if you can' by the victim's car. He's taunting the detectives and the police, and that really pisses me off," Tiegen told her.

"We'll do our parts, too, and together, we'll solve these cases and bring you the closure you need, too," Mitch told her, and she smiled.

"Together. I like the sound of that." She winked.

"Watch it, you, or we won't make it to dinner and will go straight to dessert the moment we have you alone," Mitch said, and she felt her cheeks blush.

"And that's my cue to get back to work. See you later." She headed toward the van and prepared to leave.

Chapter 7

Everything was falling into place. All the players were on the scene and leaving that note for R.J. to find had been the icing on the cake. Of course he would talk to Mia, and they would make connections in the case, and she would help. She was a kind woman, a compassionate and strong woman, and would do anything to help others. But she needed discipline when it came to giving her body to men. His earlier screw-up when he'd killed out of impatience nearly got him caught. But with R.J. wanting to protect her and maybe rekindle his feelings for her, which would keep Mia away from the three men she'd spent the weekend with, R.J. would lead her right to him. He would do all the work while Peter sat back and waited for the opportunity to strike. Killing R.J. was going to feel so good, but having Mia once and for all would be the ultimate prize. He was ready as he watched the two of them talking in the café.

* * * *

R.J. listened to Mia as she told him what she had been up to the last couple of years and about being a forensics photographer.

"Is that how you met Tiegen?" he asked her, and she held his gaze. He saw her cheeks redden a little, and he looked away and then back at her. He leaned closer over the table.

"If you're happy, then I'm happy."

"It's complicated, R.J."

"Because his brother likes you, too?" he asked.

She sighed and looked away and then straightened her shoulders and looked back at him. "I'm involved with all three of them."

R.J. was shocked. "All three of them?"

"They have a brother Murdock. He's Special Forces. I really care about them, but it's very new. Like days new." She smiled as she played with the straw wrapper from her iced tea.

"I guess I wasn't enough for you," he blurted out.

"R.J."

He held his hand up. "Forget I said that. I'm feeling sorry for myself because I let you get away. But really, you and I weren't meant to be. What we had while we had it was special. No regrets."

She smiled. "No regrets. So what about you? Any love interests?"

"No time for that with a career like mine."

"Speaking of careers, tell me more about this profile you've come up with on this killer. Why these young women with brown hair, dark eyes, and such similar attributes? Do you think it stems from this one woman, Colleen, from years ago?"

He slid over the files, and she opened them up.

"I keep racking my brain on this. Each victim sustains the same injuries, the same abuse, and it seems to mirror the death of this woman, Colleen. However, if she was the most important one, the woman that caused him to continue to kill and reenact her murder, then why leave her in woods to be found by detectives? Why not place her body somewhere he could revisit? It isn't consistent with the personality of a killer set on reenacting his crime over and over again."

Mia looked at the files she held and stared at the pictures.

"Maybe it's not the first kill, or the one he's trying to get his hands on to perform his acts and live out his fantasy with. Perhaps these were just women who resemble the specific woman he's really after?"

"We've thought about that, too, which makes this investigation and finding this guy even more difficult. He hasn't screwed up yet. Hasn't left a fiber, any DNA, no mistake we can catch."

"Well, you didn't get the result back yet from the crime scene today. That woman had a lot of blood under her nails. Perhaps she was able to scratch the killer and got some of his blood and skin under there?"

"Maybe. I suppose we'll know soon enough. Getting a clear picture of this maintenance guy or custodian or whatever he was could help, too."

"Yes, I would like to see him and maybe it would trigger a memory from the old apartment."

"That would help. You seem to be handling discussing Wynona's murder investigation well."

She took a deep breath and released it. He stared at her and couldn't help but to absorb her beauty and the way the buttons on her white blouse were undone low enough that he could catch a glimpse of her cleavage and breasts. He forced his eyes back to hers. She was taken, in a relationship with three men, and it obviously was serious.

"I guess because of my profession and because I really want to be able to help find her killer and have some closure finally. To think that this guy who is killing all these other women could be Wynona's killer, too, is crazy. I want him caught. I know you do, too, and obviously you're getting close if he's leaving a message like the one he did for you."

"Most likely it's because I was the one on the case with Wynona and then the other ones more recently. The detectives from Colleen's murder investigation have moved on and are in a new department. This is even more motivation to catch this killer."

She glanced at her watch. "I should probably head out." She'd begun to pull together the files when his cell phone rang.

"Seriously? Okay, send it through and then patch that picture to the surrounding departments. He had to be seen somewhere nearby and close to where the last woman was taken. Keep me posted." He disconnected the call and looked at Mia.

"Mosley is sending through a picture of the guy they think was the maintenance worker in all the other cases. Your boyfriend Tiegen was able to get it. Apparently he knows someone that used to be an owner of one of the apartment buildings and he kept files of employees and I.D.'s on record from years ago."

She smiled. "Great. Let's take a look." She stood up then slid into the seat next to him.

He inhaled her perfume. "Still wearing the same perfume?" he asked, and she smiled.

"You know I love it."

"I remember it well."

Their gazes locked, and then his phone beeped. He winked, and she smiled as he pulled it up.

"Here, what do you think?"

* * * *

Mia looked at the picture. There was something vaguely familiar about the man. He looked a little older, and she was certain she had never seen him at the apartment building where she and Wynona lived.

"Familiar?"

"I think so, but not from our apartment building."

Slowly she started to remember the scene from when her parents had passed and she was coming and going to the apartment before she moved out. It was scary and had been a crappy neighborhood.

"Mia?" He covered her knee with his hand.

"I remember him. Oh God, R.J., he didn't live in the building that Wynona and I rented an apartment in. He lived in my old apartment when I lived with my parents."

"What?"

"I remember the night I was out late from work and I was looking into getting another place, somewhere closer to college and in a better neighborhood. When my parents passed, this guy from social services was there. I was like nineteen, and you know, I couldn't go into any kind of foster care or anything, but he was trying to act helpful. He gave me the creeps, and one night when I came home late, he was there. He tried to get me to go out to grab a bite to eat when this guy, the one in the picture, intervened. He told the guy to get lost."

"This guy in the picture?" he asked and looked at her strangely, his eyes squinted.

"Yes. It was like he knew the guy's intention. He watched me go up the stairs and made sure I got up into the apartment safely, and then I never saw him again. The following weekend I moved out."

R.J. ran his hand over his mouth.

Mia started getting some crazy ideas and thoughts running through her head.

"Mia, we could have been wrong about this from the start. Perhaps it wasn't Wynona he was after, but you instead?"

"Me? Oh God, you think so? You think he meant to take me that night and because I worked late and Wynona was drunk that he grabbed her instead?"

"I don't know, but it seems to make sense, and if that's the case, he's somewhere nearby. He could try to go after you next and maybe he threatened me, left that note for me because he knew we were romantically involved."

She covered her mouth and pulled out her phone.

"The guys. I have to tell them. They could be in danger."

"You call them and explain what's going on. I'll drive you to their place while I call Mosley. We'll get this guy, Mia. We'll get him together."

* * * *

Mia called Tiegen's phone first. She rambled on about what was going on as she got into the unmarked police cruiser with R.J.

"We're heading to your place. Be on guard, Tiegen. This guy could want to hurt you guys to get to me."

"Jesus, Mia. We'll protect you. We'll get our friends to assist, and we'll find this guy. If he's anywhere in Wellington, Portland Place, or Yarland, we'll find him."

"Okay, Tiegen, I trust you guys. I know you'll keep me safe," she said. She ended the call and she gave directions to R.J.

"I can't believe this is happening. Wynona and these other women could have all been killed because this guy wants me." Tears filled her eyes. R.J. was taking the back roads. It was dark out, and the only lights were those of the headlights on the car as he maneuvered the tricky, winding roads.

"Don't think like that. We'll get this guy and we'll all keep you safe."

Mia gasped as something hit the car and R.J. began to lose control.

"What the fuck?" he exclaimed, and then the vehicle jerked again as another car slammed into it, sending R.J.'s vehicle into some trees and down a ravine.

"Mia," R.J. yelled out as the car tumbled over and then slammed against something hard.

She smelled the smoke and the distinct scent of transmission fluid as her head throbbed. Her arm ached terribly. She was bleeding, and her vision was fuzzy.

"R.J.?" she whispered and tried turning, but she was upside down in the car, the blood rushing to her head. The inside of the car was in complete darkness.

She heard moaning and looked over to see him there. He was unconscious, and blood oozed from his head and his nose. It was her who moaned, and it echoed. She reached around her seat, trying to gain her strength and the cognitive ability to help when she heard a creaking sound like someone opening the damaged door on R.J.'s side and then the sound of gunshots as someone shot R.J. She screamed and then heard the moaning and grunting, and a moment later arms reached in and unbuckled her belt, making her fall forward and slam against the floor and dashboard of the car. Her gun was pulled from her hip. She shoved against the hands.

"Let go. Get off of me." The blood from her head wound filled her eye, making it difficult to open it and see. She was blinded by it, and the person pulling her out knew it.

"Let's go, Mia. It's time," the voice said and dragged her from the car, over the broken glass and onto the ground. She heard phones ringing and buzzing. She grabbed for what she could, her nails and hands getting cut on the broken glass, and it hit her. Could this be the killer? The guy who might have killed Wynona and the others?

She screamed for him to let go, and he struck her. Once, twice, before lifting her over his shoulder.

"We're going, Mia. You're mine, and our new life together begins now."

Mia struggled to remain conscious, and as she fought to get him to stop walking up the embankment, he stumbled a few times but then continued, determined to get her away from the car. As he stopped, the light appeared from the back bed of a truck and large utility box. She pushed his hands from her body and tumbled against the bumper then onto the ground. She screamed out in pain as she stumbled backward on her hands, but she moved erratically, dizziness impeding her ability to escape. A moment later he hauled her up as if she weighed nothing at all and dropped her into the metal box. ,She barely fit into it. She shoved against him, begging to be let go. He slammed his fists against her body, forcing her inside. She was losing focus and strength.

"Hey, is everything all right?"

She heard the voice, sensed the headlights, and then heard the gunshots. The sound of tires squealing and then the sounds of a crash echoed behind them. She shoved her arms upward, but her body and her head were so weak. She knew this was her last chance to get away. But he was too fast as he slammed the metal top down on her arms, sending jolts of pain through her bones and flesh. She cried, and he shoved the top closed. She screamed in terror and fear and then heard the rumble of the engine and felt the motion of the truck moving. This was it. She was going to die, and her last thoughts were of R.J. and her men, who would find her dead and then have to investigate her homicide.

* * * *

It took them less than five minutes to arrive on scene. Murdock ran along the road past the many police cars, paramedics, and other responders with Tiegen and Mitch. Mitch had been speaking with Jethro and others in the department when they got the call about the car wreck and someone being shot at.

"Where is she?" Tiegen yelled to the other officers as he got closer to the wreckage.

"She's gone, Tiegen. Someone pulled her from the car," police officer Danny Voight told him.

It didn't take them long to figure out that the killer had caused the accident. R.J. was rushed to the hospital with two bullet wounds, one to his shoulder and one to his chest plus a head injury. It didn't look good. Seeing all the blood at the scene, it appeared that Mia had been dragged through the glass and had sustained injuries as well.

"So this guy pulls up in a car behind the truck and notices him carrying a woman and placing her into the back of the truck in some kind of utility box. He questions what's going on, and the guy turns and shoots at this guy, who puts his car in reverse and slams into the telephone pole. Somehow, he gets away and can't go any farther than about a half a mile down the road, where he stops and calls 911," Officer Dan Voight told them.

"Jesus. He stuffed her in a fucking box," Murdock stated angrily and ran his fingers through his hair. His brothers Mitch and Tiegen were gathering up the detectives and trying to secure the scene. In a matter of minutes, calls were coming in about this guy Peter Fayen.

"Murdock, Mitch, the feds got something." He held the phone to his ear. The others gathered around them.

"He was seen in town yesterday. Near the hardware store in Wellington. He told the clerk that he and his wife were on their honeymoon and that they were going to live their first year in a cabin in the woods and would live off the land."

"Fuck," Mitch said.

"Any indication of where this fucking cabin is?" Murdock asked.

"Not a clue and he didn't say and the store owner never asked," Tiegen told them.

They were all silent, and Murdock knew this was really bad. There wouldn't be any leads. He hadn't fucked up and left any clues or even ditched the truck.

"Mia has to be scared out of her mind," Mitch said and then ran his fingers through his hair.

"We'll find them, guys. We'll do everything we can to find Mia and get her back safe and sound," Chief Cummings said to them, but one look at everyone's faces and Murdock knew her chances of living were slim to none.

* * * *

It was four o'clock in the morning when the call came into the police department. They had set up a command center at the main station in Wellington. Every one of their friends and colleagues in law enforcement that were part of the community were there to help or be on standby for assistance. Tiegen. Mitch, Mosley, and the federal agents were organizing searches by air on the roadways. They had first centered their searches around the immediate vicinity and then began to move farther out past Yarland and into Pennsylvania in hopes of getting a clue and finding the vehicle.

Murdock sat in the chair, his head in his hands, feeling angry and exhausted. He still couldn't believe that this was happening.

But just as he started to feel the exhaustion kick in and his eyes close, someone yelled out about a sighting.

"We've got the vehicle," the federal agent called out, and Murdock jumped up.

"Where?" Nash asked.

"Pennsylvania. An hour from here."

Murdock looked at Nash and Tiegen.

"We'll take the chopper and get there faster. We'll land outside of the area just in case that cabin is within earshot," the federal agent told Tiegen.

"Let's go," Mitch said.

Murdock followed them out the door.

As they got into the SUV to get a ride to the field where the FBI helicopter would land, Murdock looked at Tiegen and Mitch.

"It's been hours."

"Listen, we don't know what we'll find at this site. It doesn't mean she's nearby, just that he ditched the truck there in the gas station."

"I understand how this works, but if he took her on foot, he wouldn't be able to carry her too far. He would have to have another means of transportation," Murdock told him.

"Could take up another vehicle," Mitch added.

"I've got some pictures coming in of the area. One of our teams is already on the scene and securing the vehicle, asking questions of local residents. It's a small town and known for summer getaways and some snowmobiling trails in the winter months. It's way up the mountains, so there could be some decreased temperatures," the agent told them. It was pretty damn cold down here in Wellington. There was a chance of snow showers all day today, so up north in the mountains was bound to be ten to fifteen degrees colder.

He didn't say a word. He didn't want to jump to conclusions and assume the worst, but he had to try to prepare himself as best he could.

"Gerry," Tiegen said to the agent in charge. He nodded toward him.

"That second set of people you have coming by helicopter following us, have them grab Damien, Elwood, and Toro Vancouver. They're amazing trackers, along with my brother Murdock. If Peter took her into the woods and the mountains, they'll help find her and quick."

The agent nodded, and Murdock typed into his cell phone, probably already in contact with Toro.

"Good idea. We don't need to waste more time when we get there waiting another thirty minutes for backup," Mitch told him.

"We need gear if we're going to track through that weather. Otherwise, none of us will be any help," Murdock said, and Tiegen's cell phone buzzed again. He smirked.

"Toro has it covered. For all of us."

* * * *

Mia was so cold she could hardly feel her hands. Her blouse was ripped open, there were cuts all over her hands, arms, and shoulders, and her head was pounding. She had to stop and vomit numerous times, but Peter was there to care for her and then push her to continue walking through the woods and up the steep inclines.

She teetered again, and he gripped her tightly. "Keep moving. We'll be there in a couple of hours.".

They had been walking all night. Or at least it felt that way once he got rid of the truck and then strapped her onto a four-wheeler to head into the woods. He seemed to have planned out everything, including where they were headed. She tried to remember aspects of the other cases, indicators as to why he'd left his victims in the wooded areas a good hour from their homes, but her head hurt so badly it was too difficult to think.

She didn't want to stop walking, or he would strike her again. Hit her like he had when she first refused to walk and get onto the four-wheeler. Her eye was swollen shut now. The blood from her head wound had dried into her eye, which made blinking sting. She shivered, and her teeth chattered. She didn't think they had gone too far because she kept having to stop to throw up or lose focus. He carried her several times, but this hill was steep. He hadn't even noticed her ripping her blouse at the pocket and leaving pieces with her blood on it. He seemed to be completely focused on getting to this cabin, this place he said would be home forever.

She smelled the snow in the air, that cold, crisp scent that made her think of the white stuff falling. Ten minutes later, as they got to another small clearing, she saw the flurries begin to fall. He chuckled.

"I couldn't have planned this better. They'll be several inches by the time we make it to the cabin."

"Several inches? We'll freeze to death," she said, teeth clattering as she stopped walking and held her arms around her waist.

"Don't stop." He shoved her, and she lost her balance and hit the ground. Her wrist twisted funny, and she felt the ache and pain as she hugged it to her chest.

"I'll take care of you. A nice hot bath, some warm new clothes I brought for you, and you'll be fine." He pulled her up and dragged her along the trail.

She thought about R.J. and hoped he was still alive. She thought about her men, and the tears filled her eyes. She had to be smart. Peter had planned this well, and finding her would be impossible. By the time they found the truck and then figured out where to look for her, she would be dead, tied to this guy's bed and raped, beaten, and murdered like the others. She needed to do something. She had to.

"Why are you doing this to me? Why did you kill the others?" she asked him.

"Because you're the one I've been waiting for."

"What do you mean?" she asked as they climbed along the rocky terrain.

"You were mine from that first moment we met. I made mistakes. They're rectified now."

She slowed down and looked around them. The snowflakes were getting heavier, thicker, as they stuck to the ground, hiding the dangers of rocks and jagged edges.

"You mean at the apartment where I lived with my parents?"

He stopped and turned to look at her. "You remember me from then?"

She nodded, and he smirked. He was creepy, his eyes dark and Charles Manson-like. His hair was jet-black with gray, indicating he was much older than her. She vaguely remembered thinking of him back then as an older man. But perhaps now he was in his fifties. He was big though. Large shoulders, big muscles, and almost as tall as Mitch.

She thought of Mitch, Murdock, and Tiegen, and she knew she wouldn't want them to find her raped and murdered in some cabin somewhere. If she was going to die and this man was going to be her maker, then she was going to die fighting.

"I remember you seemed kind. That's why I don't understand why you killed all those women. Why you're here with me now when you were protecting me from that guy back then."

"Stop talking and walk," he yelled at her and gave her another shove. She stumbled forward sliding on the slippery leaves in the woods. He pulled her along.

"We're almost home, Mia."

"It's not my home. I don't want to be here. I want to go back."

"To them?" he asked and grabbed her upper arm and started dragging her the rest of the way. As they got to the top, she saw the cabin.

"Yes to them and to my life. I don't belong here. You need help, Peter. Let me help you."

He grabbed her face and held it tightly as he looked down into her eyes.

"You are helping me. You're my woman now. You and I are going to live here forever, and no one will ever find us. Never." He pressed his lips to hers.

She shoved away from him and spat then ran her sleeve over her mouth. "No I'm not. I'm not your wife. I'm not staying here."

He struck her hard, sending her into the snow. The cold stung her bare skin along her belly and chest.

He pulled her up. "Now move it. It's been too many hours. I think we're both grumpy. We'll get inside, and I'll make us something to eat, and we'll start a fire. I have candles, too. It will be romantic, Mia. You'll see, and I'll teach you so much. You'll love your new life. I promise."

Dread filled her heart. She wasn't going to let him touch her. He would have to kill her first. That was the only way.

* * * *

Between Toro, Vancouver, Elwood, Damien, and Murdock, they were able to figure out that Peter had gotten a hold of a four-wheeler. Tracks were located by the edge of the parking lot where the gas station was and up a small trail. People living nearby said they'd heard what sounded like a four-wheeler during the night head into the woods toward the mountains. From there Tiegen and the agents got a full satellite image of the wooded area. One of the locals said that the only thing up the mountain was an abandoned old cabin from years ago. He thought he'd heard that someone purchased it but nothing more.

"The weather is getting worse up there. The weather forecast is calling for a few inches of snow, give or take. Finding their tracks is going to take longer," Toro said to them.

"Well, I say our only choice is to head in the direction of this cabin. If there isn't anything else around, then it has to be where this guy took her. It's not like he would just head with her into the woods," Damien said.

"Unless he planned on killing her now. But that doesn't add up to what R.J. and I have gathered over the months with the other cases. It seems that Mia is the one he was looking for and comparing these other women to," Mosley said.

Tiegen pulled the zipper on his jacket up and secured his weapon. The others did the same. There were groups of two, with Toro and Murdock in the lead with Tiegen and Mitch. Behind them would be the agents, plus Damien and Elwood leading the way.

"Okay, let's do this. We're losing daylight and need to move now," Toro said, and they all headed toward the woods to make the hike up the mountain.

* * * *

"Sit there," he told her as they entered the cabin, and he gave her a shove to the floor. She fell, landing on her hands, trying to stop from tumbling over. But her wrist was sprained and gave out, and she landed on her left shoulder. She cried out, but he didn't even glance at her. He started to light candles. The smell of mold, old wood, and dirt filled her nostrils. She tried to see in the darkness, now that night was falling. Combined with the snow coming down hard outside, and how high they were in the mountains, there was no sunlight, and soon it would be pitch-black out there.

She shivered on the floor, her blouse torn along the edges, and it didn't even matter. The snow would cover their path and the pieces of cloth she dropped, and that was only if they were looking for her.

He walked by and tossed a thick flannel shirt at her. She didn't care that it smelled like him. She was too cold to care. Her feet ached, her head pounded, and she wished for sleep, for rest, but she wouldn't close her eyes. God knew what he had planned for her next. As the chills and then exhaustion overtook her, she leaned her cheek against the dirty floor and closed her eyes. *I have to think of a way out of here. I have to.*

It seemed like seconds had passed when she heard something drop. She jerked upward and caught sight of him. He'd pulled some sort of cot out from the wall and was sitting on the edge of it. Then she smelled the scent of food and saw him holding a bowl and a spoon. He held her gaze with a firm, hard expression.

"Come," he said.

Her belly rumbled, the need for nourishment so great, but she didn't want to accept anything he would give her. Then she thought about it. If she ate, she would have energy, and maybe if she were smart enough, she could get away from him and run. If she tried running now on empty, she wouldn't get far, and the beating he would surely give her would send her closer to the grave.

She eased up, licked her swollen lip, and could hardly focus with her left eye. The right eye was swollen shut.

She eased closer, crawled along the floor until she was at his feet.

"Open," he said, and she opened her mouth as best she could with the cuts and swollen skin. He brought the spoon to her lips, and she drank from it. It tasted like canned soup, and he continued to feed her, in between caressing her hair and brushing his thumb along her chin.

"I wish you hadn't made me hurt you, Mia. You're too beautiful of a woman to injure."

She hoped that were the case and he wouldn't want to kill her like he had the others. Could she count on that, or would this psycho lose it and pounce?

He ate from the same spoon, and she didn't want any more. It was too intimate, too personal to share a bowl of soup with someone.

But then he gripped her jaw. "We're husband and wife now. We share everything."

She felt like throwing up. Her stomach lurched, and she swallowed down the urge to vomit.

"I need to use the bathroom."

He continued to hold her chin as he set the almost empty bowl of soup onto the bed.

He lowered closer, and she tried pulling back, but his hold was firm on her jaw.

"You use the bathroom. There's no plumbing, but I did put in a mirror and some things you might like."

She went to move, and he gripped her harder and jerked her face. She could feel the bruises under her skin.

"Say thank you," he warned.

"Thank you," she replied, and then he kissed her lips.

When he eased her body up off the floor, he escorted her to the bathroom. He wrapped his arm around her waist and pressed hard against her. He sniffed her hair, her neck, and then ran his hand up her blouse under the flannel she wore. He nipped her skin by her neck, and she tried pulling away. He squeezed her tighter.

"When you're done, we sleep."

He cupped her breast and then rocked his hips against her ass. She felt his hardened cock, and she felt the tears fill her eyes. He was going to rape her. She had to do something. She had to.

Mia got into the bathroom and closed the door. She saw the square wood seat and the darkness that led to something below the house. It wasn't the first time she'd used an outhouse, and it wasn't going to be her last. She did her business, knowing that she would need to be ready to make a move and a run for it.

She looked around the small bathroom for anything at all to use as a weapon.

She felt frantic, helpless. She knew that no one was coming for her and that she had to do this alone. She would fight him off, but her physical strength, even if she hadn't been injured, wouldn't beat a psycho like Peter.

She saw the mirror and cringed from the reflection of her face, which was battered, bruised, a mess even through the vision of one poor eye.

She buttoned the shirt. It would be her only source of heat against the elements if she got away.

She searched in the cabinet, and there was nothing but a brush, some hairbands, a bottle of perfume—her favorite, the sick fuck. She pulled it out. She reached for the mirror, pulled the small frame off the wall, and then placed it onto the floor. She put the towel over the mirror and then stomped on the towel. The sound was thankfully soft enough not to alert him as to what she was doing.

She lifted the towel and saw the large, sharp piece. She pulled it out, grabbed some toilet paper, wrapped it around the bottom so she wouldn't cut herself, and then she pulled the top off the perfume bottle. She gave one spray, confirming it worked.

"Let's do this, Mia. You had a good run. Let's go out fighting," she whispered to herself and then opened the bathroom door.

* * * *

"What's this?" Toro said as they got higher up the mountain and began to hit the snow covering the ground.

"That's my girl," Murdock said as he looked at it and smelled Mia's perfume.

"It's Mia's?" Tiegen asked.

"Sure the fuck is. Smell it." He passed it to Tiegen, and Tiegen smiled.

"She left it on purpose. We have to be headed in the right direction," Murdock said.

"Who the hell is this woman?" Elwood asked him.

"She's our woman. She's resourceful, and she knows how this guy thinks. Either way she wants to be certain we find them and he's captured. We need to move," Murdock said, and they continued up. The farther they went, the more they came across, despite the snow. Another bloody piece of blouse, some blood, and he knew she was fighting to live."

"This is a long fucking way to make her walk if she was injured in the car accident," Toro said to them.

"She's tough. She has a black belt in Tae Kwon Do, knows how to use weapons, and graduated top in her class, plus the position she has with the BCI Unit and coroner's office was created just for her," the agent told them.

"I'm not surprised," Mitch said, and they continued to go farther up.

"We should keep these flashlights down just in case he's keeping watch," the agent said.

"Once we get to that hill, the cabin should be another hundred yards up. We'll use the night vision glasses," Damien told them, and they continued on their path.

Keep on fighting, Mia. We're coming, baby. We're coming. Murdock clenched his teeth and trudged on through the snow, his weapon cocked and ready.

* * * *

She opened the door and hid her weapons. At first she didn't see him, and she looked toward where they'd come in and the large wooden door by the sitting area.

But as she got closer, he appeared in front of her, wearing no shirt and covered with scars.

"I've waited so long for this night. To hold you in my arms and make love to you, Mia."

"Keep on waiting, asshole." She pulled the perfume out and sprayed him in the eyes. He roared in anger and reached for her, gripping her shirt and pulling her toward him. She stabbed him with the piece of mirror, right in the shoulder and neck area. He released her and stumbled back. She gave him a kick and a punch, knocking him to the ground, and he reached for the gun.

She kicked it from his hand, but it went behind him.

She ran for the door, pulled it open, shocked at how pitch-black it was, but she ran anyway.

She was crying but trying to be quiet. There was no way he could see her. She just needed to run. She placed her hands out in front of her. The snow was smacking against her cheeks and neck, stinging her cheeks, but she tried to remember the direction they'd come in and how long the clearing was. Then she thought about him using the gun and shooting her. She needed cover. She ran to the left and nearly hit the tree, but with her hands in front of her, they hit first. She slowed her pace, only because she didn't want to knock herself out by smacking into a tree. Her vision was poor with her injuries, her head throbbing from the concussion and her wrist throbbing from the sprain. She didn't need to knock herself out.

She heard the roaring in the distance. He was yelling her name, and then she heard the gunshots. One ricocheted past her head and hit the tree in front of her. She ducked and fell to the ground, soaking her dress pants with wet snow.

She was walking slowly, trying not to give her location up, when she sensed the change in the ground below her feet. It was too late when she realized it was the steep decline, and she tumbled down, trying not to scream as her body hit numerous branches and rocks. Finally a tree against her ribs stopped her.

She was stuck in the snow, now covered all over and feeling numb, nauseous as her head spun and she lost all ability to feel her body. This was it. She was going to die right here, and she knew it. But she'd gotten away from him.

She fought with her mind to not give up and to keep fighting. But what was the use? She was miles from the road, injured so badly she couldn't even move, and soon hypothermia would set in and finish her off.

* * * *

They heard the gunshots and saw the spark from the barrel of the gun shooting into the woods. They all took cover and used their night vision glasses and waited to see where Mia was.

Tiegen watched, clearly noticing that Peter had no shirt and was holding his neck and shoulder as he pointed the gun to his left, their right, and fired into the woods.

"Mia!" He screamed out her name, and they knew that somehow Mia had gotten away.

"Take him out," Tiegen said, and Murdock took the shot from the distance.

Peter fell to the ground, and everyone approached with caution.

As they descended upon the body and the cabin, they searched quickly for Mia, after making sure that Peter was no longer a threat.

"He reeks like perfume," the one agent said as he checked Peter's injuries.

"It looks like she sprayed him with it and stabbed him with a piece of mirror from the bathroom." Damien pointed to the floor and the bloody piece of mirror.

"She got away. She's out there somewhere and can't be far. This just happened." Murdock started to head to the front and look around.

"Here, fresh footprints," Toro told them.

"Good eye," Tiegen said, and Murdock, Tiegen, Mitch, Toro, Damien, and Elwood headed in search of Mia. The agents remained behind and called in for assistance.

"Jesus, where the hell could she be?" Mitch asked as they slowly followed the footprints.

"Mia! Mia, where are you?" Tiegen yelled out her name, but they heard nothing. In the distance, they could hear the sound of four-wheelers making their way up the mountain. That would be their ride down, and they would be taking Mia with them. He wasn't leaving here without her.

"Look, watch yourself, that's a steep drop," Toro told them, stopping them right before the steep incline.

"Oh shit." Tiegen slid to his ass. They all noticed the same thing at the same time. Mia, lying in the snow, unconscious.

Murdock pulled off his night vision goggles, and Toro and his brothers lit up the area with flares.

"Oh God, look at her. Look what he fucking did to her." Mitch reached for her shirt to check the damage.

"Head injury. The blood is dry though so maybe from the accident. We need to get her warm," Elwood said, and Tiegen slowly lifted her up and into his arms as Murdock looked at her belly and ribs.

"I think she has some broken ribs," Murdock told them.

"Let's wrap her up tight so when we take her down on the four-wheeler, the bumping around won't injure her more," Toro suggested, and Damien pulled out a special plastic blanket to wrap her with. It would keep her body warm.

As they started to wrap her up, she began to moan. Murdock placed his hand against her cheek. "You're safe, Mia. We've got you, baby. It's over."

She moaned, and he held her close as they made their way down the mountain to the safest spot a four-wheeler could meet them and make the rest of the trip down.

"Murdock?" she whispered.

"Yes, baby. We've got you."

"You came," she whispered and then cringed.

"We told you we would never leave you, never abandon you, baby, and we meant it."

"We love you, Mia," Tiegen told her.

"We sure do, baby." Mitch added, and she closed her eyes, and they got her to safety together.

Epilogue

Mia slowly made her way out of the bedroom and toward the staircase. She was tired of lying in bed resting. She needed to move around. She'd never been laid up before, and she hated it.

As she grabbed onto the railing and took the first step, she tightened up. Three weeks had passed, and her ribs were still sore, her head still ached, but her vision was finally almost perfect. Still, she was aching everywhere. She had cuts and bruises on every part of her body and suffering from hypothermia had lasting effects she was still getting over.

Before she reached the next step, Mitch was in front of her, holding on to her hips.

"What in God's name do you think you're doing, Mia?" he scolded, and she exhaled and tried to continue walking alone down the stairs.

"This is not happening."

"Please, Mitch. Let me do this. I can't stand lying in bed. I need to move around. I'm getting all flabby and weak."

He hugged her close and ran his hand down the back of her sweatpants and squeezed her ass. "You don't feel flabby to me."

She smiled then leaned her forehead against his shoulder.

"What's going on here?" Murdock asked, joining the conversation from the bottom of the stairs.

"Nothing. We're just coming downstairs for breakfast, that's all."

"Oh really? Because it looks like you were trying to sneak down the stairs without assistance and Mitch caught you."

"I need to do this, Murdock. I'm not used to lying around and being lazy."

She continued to walk down the stairs, and with each step, her muscles felt better and better. She was ready to start getting things back to normal. That thought made her wonder when the guys might want her to go back to her place. When she got to the bottom step, Murdock was there to pull her into his arms and then kissed her deeply.

He ran his hand over her ass and then gave it a slap. "You're in great shape, baby, but your body still needs rest."

"I'm done. I want to be able to go see R.J. this weekend. The bruises on my face are better, and I won't look like some freak when we go out to dinner in the city."

They walked her into the kitchen. Tiegen was placing pancakes and bacon onto the table.

"Look who we found coming down the stairs all alone," Murdock said, tattling on her.

"What?" Tiegen asked, eyes squinted and a spatula in his hand. "Mia?"

"Oh cool it, Tiegen. I'm being a burden, and there's no need for it. I'm better now. I swear. In fact, we should talk about my apartment. I need to go back soon and get things back to normal."

"It's not necessary," Murdock told her.

"What do you mean?" she asked as Tiegen made her a plate and Mitch poured her coffee, making it like she liked it, black.

"What is that supposed to mean? I thought that we could stop by there today so I can see what dresses I have to wear for Saturday when we meet R.J. in the city."

She popped a piece of bacon into her mouth.

"You're not moving back to the apartment, Mia. We want you here with us," Tiegen told her, and Murdock joined them by the table.

She swallowed hard. "What are you saying?"

"We're saying that we love you and want to spend every day with you," Tiegen replied.

"We want to look into your eyes before we go to sleep at night," Mitch said.

"And see your beautiful face, and feel your sexy body pressed up against ours every morning," Murdock added.

"But I'm safe now. I know what I went through was traumatic for all of us, but I'm fine." She felt the tears reach her eyes. She wasn't fine. She was in love with these guys, and she didn't want to live without them or leave them. How could she survive without them?

"You're a strong, smart, beautiful woman, and we want you in our house, in our bed, and right where you belong, here with us."

"Don't you love us like we love you, Mia?" Tiegen asked her.

She smiled, and a tear leaked from her eye.

"I love you more than anything in the whole world. You've filled a hole in my heart I've had forever, and no one could replace the three of you. When I was lost, hurt, and had nearly given up the fight to live, you showed up. You didn't abandon me like all the other people in my life. I don't want to move out and go back to living alone. I need the three of you. I want to be here. I guess I just needed you to tell me you wanted me here with you forever and that you loved me like I love you."

"Then it's settled. Because with you is where the three of us belong. Eat your breakfast, because then it's back to bed and making love for the rest of day," Tiegen told her then brought her hand to his lips and kissed the top of it.

"Besides, now that I'm retired from the service, who is going to keep me occupied?" Murdock asked and winked, and Mitch chuckled.

"There's always the opening in the police department in Wellington," he said to him.

"Maybe I'll look into it." Murdock leaned over and kissed Mia on the lips. She placed her hand against his cheek and smiled.

"You'd make a good police officer and detective, Murdock, plus your ass would look mighty fine in uniform." She used her free hand to tap his ass.

Mitch and Tiegen chuckled.

"Oh you just wait until after breakfast, baby. That sexy ass is due for a few spankings."

She gasped as he cupped her breast, gave it a squeeze, and pulled away.

She couldn't help but to smile just thinking about making love to her three men together. She was blessed to have met them, to have met three men who made her feel safe and had taught her to take the chance and let her heart lead the way. She trusted them with her life, with her heart, and definitely with her body.

She smiled to herself and felt the hum of desire and need for her men. For when they were all together, all connected as one, she felt whole and important, instead of that lonely girl with a wall around her heart and a fear she thought would never go away. That wasn't the case anymore because, when she had been at a crossroads and needed to decide to take a chance and let her heart lead the way or run away from the feelings she had, she'd taken a chance. She would never regret doing so with Tiegen, Murdock, and Mitch McKay.

THE END

WWW.DIXIELYNNDWYER.COM

ABOUT THE AUTHOR

People seem to be more interested in my name than where I get my ideas for my stories from. So I might as well share the story behind my name with all my readers.

My momma was born and raised in New Orleans. At the age of twenty, she met and fell in love with an Irishman named Patrick Riley Dwyer. Needless to say, the family was a bit taken aback by this as they hoped she would marry a family friend. It was a modern day arranged marriage kind of thing and my momma downright refused.

Being that my momma's families were descendants of the original English speaking Southerners, they wanted the family blood line to stay pure. They were wealthy and my father's family was poor.

Despite attempts by my grandpapa to make Patrick leave and destroy the love between them, my parents married. They recently celebrated their sixtieth wedding anniversary.

I am one of six children born to Patrick and Lynn Dwyer. I am a combination of both Irish and a true Southern belle. With a name like Dixie Lynn Dwyer it's no wonder why people are curious about my name.

Just as my parents had a love story of their own, I grew up intrigued by the lifestyles of others. My imagination as well as my need to stray from the straight and narrow made me into the woman I am today.

Enjoy *Crossroads 4: Shot Through the Heart* and allow your imagination to soar freely.

For all titles by Dixie Lynn Dwyer, please visit
www.bookstrand.com/dixie-lynn-dwyer

Siren Publishing, Inc.
www.SirenPublishing.com

Lightning Source UK Ltd.
Milton Keynes UK
UKHW02f1127290118
316997UK00011B/649/P

9 781682 957905